From the Chicken House

Black water does it for me. Not seeing the bottom but sensing movement below, the reeds pulling at your feet. And then there's the power of water, suddenly transforming our towns and villages. What if something or someone began to direct that power for a dark purpose? Whatever you do, don't read Rachel Ward's brilliant new thriller in the bath – especially if you've got a dripping tap ...

Barry Cunningham
Publisher

THE
DROWNING
RACHEL WARD

2 Palmer Street, Frome, Somerset BA11 1DS

Text © Rachel Ward 2013
First published in Great Britain in 2013
The Chicken House
2 Palmer Street
Frome, Somerset BA11 1DS
United Kingdom
www.doublecluck.com

Cover design and interior design by Steve Wells
Cover photo by Rosie Hardy
Typeset by Dorchester Typesetting Group Ltd
Printed and bound in Great Britain by CPI Group (UK) Ltd, Croydon, CR0 4YY

The paper used in this Chicken House book is made from wood grown in sustainable
forests.

1 3 5 7 9 10 8 6 4 2

British Library Cataloguing in Publication data available.

Paperback ISBN 978-1-908435-36-1
E-book ISBN 978-1-908435-79-8

This is for Ozzy, Ali and Pete —
who help to keep my head above water.

Foreword

The idea for this book came from a story told to my husband by one of his colleagues, who had been struck by lightning when swimming in a lake with two friends. The lightning disappeared from my story, but the idea of three people in a lake stuck. I wrote the book on sabbatical from my day job, and it turned into a sort of twisted love letter to the town I worked in for ten years. I need to be clear that this is not a book about that town, or any of the people I've met there. Neither was it directly inspired by tragic events that happened in the UK and beyond during a very rainy 2012. Unfortunately drowning is incredibly common and as I was writing I became painfully aware of the loss brought to families through drowning accidents and the tragic effects of floods. I don't wish to add to anyone's pain, but I do write about real issues that affect people every day. If you've been affected by drowning, or flooding, then maybe this isn't the book for you. For everybody else, I hope that you enjoy this ... and that maybe it sends a little shiver down your spine.

Rachel Ward
Bath, November 2012

Prologue

'Stop. We need to stop. That's it, everyone — we've done our best. I'm calling it. It's four seventeen.'

I open my eyes. A raindrop hits my left eye, dead centre. I shut both eyes quickly. Careful now, I squint out. The rain keeps coming. Water bombs dropping out of a grey sky. There's stuff in my mouth. Mud. Gravel.

I turn my head and spit.

There's a face a metre from mine. Hair plastered on to his forehead in glistening snakes. Mouth, thin lips slightly apart, a trickle of water spilling out of the corner. Pale skin, streaked with mud. Eyes, closed, stunted eyelashes forming two stubby lines.

It's my face.

Something buzzes from his feet up his legs, past his waist, up to his shoulders. The hand tugging on the zip pauses for a second and then finishes the job, closing the bag right up. A sleeping bag. They've put him in a sleeping bag, 'cos he's asleep. But there's no gap in this bag. They've sealed him in. How's he going to breathe?

They'll do me next. I know they will. But I'm not asleep. I'm awake.

'Don't zip me in.' I can hear the words in my head, but my lips aren't moving. 'Don't zip me.' My voice, trying to get out, strangled in my throat.

Someone grabs my legs. Someone else grabs my arms. It's my turn. They're going to put me in a bag. They're going to zip me in. I try to put up a fight, but my arms and legs are just too heavy. I can't do a thing. Can't move, can't speak, can't think straight.

I'm on some sort of board now, being bumped off the ground and into a van. The doors slam shut. We're leaving him behind.

But no, the door's yanked open again. That'll be him now. Footsteps, grunts, as they lift him in. I look across. If the bag's still done up, I'll try to find my voice, ask them to unzip him a bit, so I can see his face, so he can get some air.

But it's not him. There's a girl in here now. She's looking right at me. Her make-up's smeared down her face from her eyes, like she's melting, but her lips are blue, her arms are covered in goosebumps and she's shivering. She's staring too, staring at me, then she blinks – once, twice – and starts screaming.

ONE

The woman who says she's my mum gets a cab to take us home. She sits one side, I sit the other side, like we're clinging to the windows. Forty centimetres of plastic seat between us. Seat belts on.

The smell in here keeps catching the back of my throat. Smells like plastic and polish and vomit all mixed up. There's a little blue tree dangling from the front mirror. It's got 'New Car Scent' printed on it. If that's what a new car smells like, you can keep it.

Home. I can't picture it, but I know that I don't want to go there. I want to go back to the hospital. That nurse was kind to me, not like the woman on the other side of this car, the one in the shiny tracksuit that's too big for her, who looks as though she's cried so hard she's worn herself out. She doesn't look like she wants to be with me any more than I want to be with her. She can hardly look at me, and she hasn't said a word, her lips clamped shut, locked together in a grim, thin line.

I'll go back. Shall I? Shall I do it? Yank the handle and kick the door open? Jump out and start running? Too late. The cab turns a corner and accelerates, and the hospital's gone.

I'm trapped.

I press my forehead against the window. It's cold against my skin. I like the feeling, it's soothing. I roll my face forwards, pressing as much of it as I can on to the smooth, hard glass, squashing my nose sideways so my mouth and chin can make contact. I press harder, my lips spreading like two slugs. The woman glances at me with red-rimmed eyes.

'What are you doing?' she says. 'Stop it, Carl, for goodness' sake.'

She reaches across the gap and tugs at my arm. I resist. She lets go and slaps me hard across the back of my head. The force of her hand makes my face skid forwards on the spitty glass, smearing my cheek. And instantly I get echoes of all the other times she's hit me, stretching back like a hall of mirrors. She retreats to the other side of the cab, tears running down her face. And I know it's true, what they've all been saying. She is my mum. My stomach falls down inside me as broken memories cartwheel through my head. Her hair scraped back. The smell of beer on her breath. The sting of her hand on my skin. Raised voices. A man shouting. A woman screaming. Slamming doors. Other memories too, a whole mess of them I can't get hold of yet. But one thing's certain.

4

She's my mum. She's the only one I've got. I don't know if I love her or hate her, if I'm scared of her or sorry for her.

I move away from the window and wipe my face on my sleeve.

'Look at the mess on there. Chrissake, how old are you? Your brother's just died. Can't you have some respect?'

How old am I? I don't even know that.

She scrubs away her tears. 'Fifteen-year-olds don't do that sort of thing, for God's sake.'

I shake my head, trying to shake away the tears of my own that are threatening to spill out. And now I hear a voice in my head, saying over and over: *Don't let her see you cry. If she sees you cry, she's won. Boys don't cry, Cee.* I blink hard, bite my lip and turn away from her towards the window.

The world we're driving through looks so normal. There are shops and houses and cars and people. I don't recognise any of it. We pass some big houses and I wonder if any of them is ours, but somehow I know that they aren't. Why can't I remember? Out of the town, we pass villages strung out along the road and then head into another, smaller town, going by a big brick factory on the outskirts. I look glumly at the takeaways and charity shops and boarded-up windows in the high street. There's an A-board on the pavement outside a newsagent's. We're past too quickly for me to read the first side, so I crane round and catch the words on the second: 'LAKE TRAGEDY: LATEST'.

An old woman pushes a trolley past the sign. She's wearing slippers.

'Nearly there,' Mum says as we head out of the high street and into an estate. Three minutes later we're turning round the back of a parade of shops and coming to a halt. The meter's showing £12.60. Mum gets her purse out of her bag. She finds a tenner and then digs about for the coins.

'There's one, two,' she says, 'and twenty, thirty, Christ I can't get my fingers on the bloody things.' She's down to coppers now, scrabbling in the purse's lining, taking her hand out, examining the coins and digging in again. And now I notice the tip of the little finger on her right hand is missing. No fingertip, no nail – it just stops at the last joint. And I know she wasn't born that way, but I can't remember how she lost it. Someone told me once ... someone told me. 'Forty-two. Forty-four.' She's not got it. She's not got enough.

The guy looks at her without emotion. He's just waiting for his cash – anyone can see she's not getting there – but it's like he wants her to say it. And in the end, she has to.

'I ain't got it,' she says. 'Twelve forty-seven. That's all I've got.'

He looks at her steadily for a minute and then decides he's better off without us. Suddenly he can't wait to get rid.

'Just give it here,' he says and holds his hand out.

The car's already moving as I'm closing the door. The tyres squeal as he makes his getaway.

'Now I've got to find my bloody keys.' Mum's rooting about in her bag again. We're at the bottom of some

6

concrete steps. 'You go up,' she says. 'I'm right behind you.'

I look up at the short flight of steps that leads to a walkway. A picture flashes into my mind. A boy who looks like me clattering down the steps and vaulting over the wall. And someone else, waiting where I am now – a girl with long dark hair. I play the scene over and over, see him flying over the wall like Batman, see her looking up, see the smile playing at the side of her mouth. She's trying not to show she's impressed, but she is. The boy. The girl. I know them, but it's not all slotting into place. He must be my brother. Must be.

The pictures in my head are like cobwebs strung across the steps. Fragile. I don't want to walk through and break them. I don't want them to go. I want to stand here and watch until it all makes sense. Until I *feel* it. It'll come, I know it will. It's there, like a word on the tip of my tongue. If I just stand and watch ...

Mum barges past me.

'Found them,' she says. 'Come on. I need a drink.'

I'm still staring at the steps, but now Mum's on them, walking up slowly, and the spell's broken. Her jogger bottoms are too long, the hems scuffed where they drag on the floor. She turns round at the top of the steps.

'Get up here, Carl.' She jerks her head to emphasise her words, and then stands staring down at me. She's waiting. 'Carl?'

'Mum, I ...'

'What's the matter? Get up here. Let's get inside. Have a drink and forget this God-awful day for a bit.'

I drag myself up the steps towards her. She's playing with the keys in her hand, looking at them, instead of me. I'm here now, but she's not moving.

'Mum,' I say.

She still doesn't look up. Her head is down, straggly bleached hair falling either side of her face. Her parting is a zigzag, startlingly pink against dark roots. Something splashes on her fingers. And again. She makes a strangled noise in her throat. Oh God, she's crying again. I try to say something to make her stop.

'Mum. Don't. It's all right.'

Somehow it was easier when she was shouting at me. This is worse, much worse.

I'm not tall, but I'm taller than her. I could put my arm round her shoulders, but all I can think of is the slap she gave me in the taxi.

Her tears are dropping on to the concrete now. She's just standing there, small and alone, fiddling with her keys, crying. And it's awful, just awful. I've got to do something.

I shuffle closer to her and lift my arm up. I keep it hanging in the air, a few inches away from her, then I gently bring it down to rest across the top of her back. I curve my fingers round so I'm holding her shoulder. At first she doesn't react and I feel stupid, awkward, but just as I'm about to move my arm away, she tips her head sideways towards me. Only a little bit, but the top of her head touches my jaw. I don't know what to do. I let go of her shoulder and pat her back a couple of times.

She moves her head back and sniffs hard.

'You do it,' she says, her words all blurry so I can only just make them out, and she hands the keys to me. They're all wet from her tears. I wipe them on my top and set off along the walkway. Each maisonette has got a fenced-off bit between the walkway and the door, like its own little yard. There's a couple of rabbit hutches at number 1, bright plastic toys scattered all over the place, a trike on its side. Number 2's got nothing, just one bin in an empty space. The next one's got as much rubbish on the floor as in the bin; bottles, a couple of them smashed, cans. There's two plastic chairs, which I'm guessing used to be white, one of them with a wonky leg, and an old armchair with the stuffing coming out. There are flowers as well. Heaps and heaps of flowers in plastic wrappers, piled up by the door. That's how I know it's our place.

The flowers are for my brother who drowned. They've told me over and over, but it's just a story. Something that happened to someone else. I can't remember a thing. They said my memory will come back, but it's hard to believe when you can't even remember where you live.

I stop by the gate. Mum comes and stands next to me and we gawp at our front yard.

'I didn't know he had that many friends,' Mum says weakly.

I push at the gate and go up to the door, sweeping a path through the flowers with my feet. Some of them have got little cards stapled to the plastic, with handwritten messages.

'Don't kick 'em,' Mum says. She's following behind, picking them up.

I put the key up to the lock. My hand's shaking. I open the door and let Mum go in first, her arms full of flowers. I scoop up the ones she's missed and walk into the hall. The place smells stale: stale drink and stale smoke. I follow her into a kitchen; mottled grey plastic worktops, grey cupboard doors and a little table pushed up against the wall.

She drops the flowers in a heap on the floor and heads for the fridge. From the doorway I can see that the contents are two six-packs of lager, half a pint of milk, a bottle of ketchup and another of brown sauce.

Mum takes a can out and cracks it open, tipping her head back and pouring it in. Her throat pulses as she swallows mouthful after mouthful until it's all gone. She reaches for another. 'Do you want one?' She holds a can out towards me.

'All right,' I say. Anything to dull the misery of coming back to this dump. I put the flowers I'm holding on the table and take the can. I pop the top and take a swig. The bitter taste fills my mouth and trips another switch in my head. *Lounging on some grass, with water lapping near my feet. The boy's there, the one that looks like me, we're drinking ourselves silly, T-shirts off to catch the sun. I can feel the warmth of it on my face and my shoulders, the itchiness of the grass on my elbow where I'm propping myself up. He takes a long drag on a cigarette and blows the smoke towards the lake.*

There's a lump in my throat. Feels like I'm going to be sick. I swallow hard, forcing the drink down. Mum's sucking on her second tube of lager like her life depends on it. She finishes it and puts the empty on the side. The fridge is still open. She reaches forward.

'You can have this,' I say, holding my nearly-full can towards her.

'No, that's yours. It's all right.'

She's got another one now and she starts necking it like the last two. She's going to be out of it soon. I'm holding my can but I'm not drinking any more. I'm just watching.

'Mum ...'

I want to stop her, tell her about the sun and the water. I want to ask her about the boy. The boy who could fly through the air and land on his feet like a cat.

My brother.

Rob.

'What?' she says.

'Can we ... can we just talk?'

She glances at me and then quickly away. She looks trapped, cornered. Like the idea of talking makes her scared.

'I'm tired, Carl. It's been a hell of a ... Let me have a drink. We'll talk later, I promise,' she says.

'But ...'

'Don't start, Carl, I need this,' she snaps, her voice brittle, close to breaking, close to tears. I don't want her to cry again so I stand aside as she heads into the front room. She settles on the sofa, one can in her hand, the others on the floor next to her, within reach. I hang around in the doorway. She doesn't look at me or try to talk to me.

'Mum,' I say, after a few minutes. She's going to get trashed and I don't even know where my bedroom is.

She looks up, startled, like she'd forgotten I was even there.

'What?'

'Where do I sleep?'

She scrunches up her eyes, trying to work out what I mean.

'Your room,' she says, in a tone that says I'm an idiot. Case closed. End of. She turns away, back to the telly that isn't on. I can't stand being here with her any more. There obviously aren't any bedrooms down here, so I head upstairs, but get stuck halfway. This should be easy – walking upstairs and into a room. Nothing to it. Just one foot in front of the other.

But it feels like trespassing, walking round someone else's house.

Now I'm looking up and I can see three doors and my legs just stop. One of them's got three holes in it. For a moment, I'm staring at them, wondering how they got there, but then I hear the noise when Rob punched them there. *One, two, three – fists balled up tight and him in a total fury. Then, in a flash, he turns back to me and his fist flies into my face.*

I turn round, sit down and take a swig from the can that I've still got in my hand.

What was he so mad about?

Another mouthful. And another. It's me and the beer and the stairs and the dark. I sit and drink until it's all gone. The liquid's heavy in my stomach but it's doing its job. I feel softer round the edges. I feel tired too, could do with a lie down. Come on, Carl. I leave my empty can on the step, swing on to my feet and head upstairs, trailing my hands on the walls either side. The surface is bobbly under my fingers. There's something comforting about the woodchip lumps and bumps. How many times have I done this, felt these walls? Is this what I do when I walk upstairs?

I go along the landing past the first door. It's open. There's a double bed, women's clothes strewn around the floor, bottles and tubes and all sorts of make-up littering the top of a scruffy chest of drawers. The next door is the bathroom. I move on and stop in front of the final door. I close my fingers and put my fist in one of the holes in the door. There's space around it. He was bigger than me. My big brother.

I push the door open and go in.

TWO

The stale smell fills my head. I can't tell what it smells of, but it floods me with feelings, things half remembered. There are two mattresses lying parallel to each other, along the walls with a metre or so in between. And not much else. Clothes lying about. Some magazines. Empty cans. A couple of fishing rods propped in a corner.

Two mattresses, no pillows, no sheets like in the hospital, just sleeping bags on the top. One orange and one green. The green one's mine. How do I know that? I sit down on top of it, then, with nothing else to do, I climb inside, shoes on and everything. I pull the nylon edges up with both hands, so I've just got my eyes and nose sticking out. I'm lying on my side, looking across the room and at Rob's mattress, his orange sleeping bag crumpled up in a heap.

And now I can hear the zip ripping up past his face and over the top of his head. See his face, streaked with mud – there one minute, gone the next. Sealed in.

I close my eyes and I'm underwater. *There's a tangle of arms and legs, thrashing in front of me. The water's pressing down, my lungs are hurting, an ache that's turning into a pain. I can't breathe. I've got to get some air. I've got to …*

I open my eyes and it's just me in this dirty jumble of a room. I'm breathing hard, and the air coming in and out of me feels like it's second-hand. It leaves a sour taste on my tongue. I think back to my hospital room – how bright, white and clean it was. It smelled of antiseptic. Now I push my nose into the fabric of the sleeping bag and inhale. It's the stale smell of old sweat. It disgusts me, but there's something reassuring about it too. This is me. It must be – it's my sleeping bag. This is how I smell.

But who am I? And who was my brother? Did I like him? Did he like me? Not if the memory on the stairs was anything to go by.

I think about what they told me, 'Your brother's dead. There was an accident. He drowned.' Why I don't feel a thing? I must be a monster, not to feel sad.

I lie still for a while. It's dark now, but there's light from the landing coming in through the open door. I look and listen, trying to take it all in – this place. Home. The place is quiet, no noise from downstairs, but I can hear the TV going next door, and people walking in the street outside, cars coming and going, doors slamming. There's a dark patch on the ceiling in the corner above Rob's mattress. There's scribble on the walls.

I feel like I've landed from another planet, been dropped into someone else's life and left to get on with it. I want to go back to the hospital. This place isn't mine. The woman downstairs isn't my mum. The boy who died wasn't my brother. There's been a mistake, a terrible, terrible mistake.

I'm shaking now. I'm scared. I can't handle this. I don't want to be here.

My nose catches that smell again, the smell a body leaves in a place when it's slept there night after night. And it tells me I'm wrong. This place is mine. There's no getting away from it.

I wrap my arms around myself and curl up tighter in my sleeping bag, but I still can't relax. Without thinking I unwind one of my arms and reach under my mattress, and my fingers close around something hard and flat. I pull it out. In the soft light I see the cover of a hardback book. The letters in the title are large, white against black: *Of Mice and Men*. Lying on my side I open it up and find the first page. The light isn't good enough for me to make out the type, but I don't need to see it, the words come to me from somewhere in the fog of my brain: 'A few miles south of Soledad, the Salinas river drops in close to the hillside bank and runs deep and green. The water is warm, too, for it has slipped twinkling over the yellow sands in the sunlight before reaching the narrow pool.'

'*For fuck's sake, Cee, turn the bloody light out.*'

'*I'm still reading.*'

'*You've read that thing six hundred times.*'

'*So?*'

'So put the bloody light out. I'm knackered.'

Holding the book close to my chest, still cocooned in my sleeping bag, I wriggle across the floor until my face is hovering over Rob's mattress, his orange sleeping bag. I rest down, breathing hard. The material under my nose is rank, as rank as mine, only different. I shut my eyes again and I can hear him breathing.

'Say goodnight, Cee,' he says. And I know that this is what he does every night. Did. This is what he did.

He'd tell me to say goodnight first and I'd say, 'Night, Rob,' back.

And he'd say, 'Night, Cee.'

Every night.

I say it now, 'Night, Rob,' and I keep my eyes closed, my body lying in the gap between our beds, my head on his mattress.

His breathing is steady and slow and I find myself breathing in time with him. The book falls to the floor and I'm drifting. Drifting slowly off to sleep.

THREE

I wake up in a dark, quiet space. I've got no idea where I am, what time it is, who I am. And then, slowly, it comes back to me.

My name is Carl Adams.

I'm fifteen.

My brother's dead.

The last thought rattles round my head. Rob's dead. Rob's dead. I know it's huge, but it's only words, just words.

I remember falling asleep here, hearing his breathing, his voice. There's nothing now. No noise from outside, no telly playing. Only a tap dripping somewhere in the flat. It's a faint sound, but everywhere's so quiet now I can definitely hear it – and my mind focuses on it. Plip, plip, plip. Like seconds ticking away on a clock.

The top of the sleeping bag is wet where I've dribbled

in my sleep. I move it away from me, sit up and wipe my mouth on the back of my hand. My head's achy and my throat's dry. I struggle out of the bag and stumble on to the landing. The light's still on. I head for the bathroom door, where the dripping sound's coming from.

It's the cold tap at the sink. I turn it full on, bend forward, cup my hands and splash water on to my face. *A boy shouts. A girl screams. Water's in my face, my eyes, my ears. My heart's racing. I'm close to them now, so close I can see their arms and legs thrashing, see his jaw clenched with the effort, her face contorted with terror.*

I jump back from the sink and reach around blindly for a towel. My hand finds the pull cord for the light, I tug at it and the light clicks on. I grab a towel from the floor and frantically rub at my face, then stare round the room. There's no one here. It's only a small room; sink, toilet, bath with a shower at one end and a plastic shower curtain bunched up. Black mould between the tiles, and on the ceiling. My heart's still beating ten to the dozen in my chest.

I was there, in the lake. I was there when my brother died.

I take a few deep breaths, sucking the cold, damp air deep into me, trying to calm down.

The tap's still running, gushing full pelt into the sink, gurgling down the waste pipe. I don't want it on my face, in my eyes, but I am thirsty. I turn the top round, cutting the flow to something a bit more than a trickle. I lean over again and hang my head under carefully, turning my face so I can catch the water in my mouth.

It's cold and clean. I swish it round, squirting it between my teeth, slooshing it over my gums, inside my puffed-out cheeks, then I spit. I swallow the next mouthful and the next, feeling the cool freshness make its way down inside me. I'm ragingly thirsty – the more water I drink, the worse it seems to get. I reach up and increase the flow as I gulp and swallow and gulp some more. Water spills out of my mouth, down my chin and my cheek.

Cee.

Someone says my name – not like the shouting and splashing that I heard before – this is close, here, in this room. I stand up, turn the tap off and look behind me. There's no one. I shake my head, dig the corner of the towel into my ears to get the water out.

It sounded like ... but it couldn't be. I heard him last night, though, when I was drifting off. But that's different, isn't it? When you're nearly asleep, the edges blur, you're halfway into your dreams, aren't you? But I'm awake now. The cold water's seen to that.

Someone's messing about, playing tricks on me.

I take two paces across the room and yank the plastic shower curtain right back. The bath is empty. This room is empty. But there was someone ... I heard someone.

I go on to the landing, stop for a minute and listen. It's quiet. Somewhere in the distance, a siren is howling, but even that fades and disappears. I head towards Mum's room.

I walk softly inside. It's not as dark as mine. The curtains are open and the streetlight outside is casting a yellow glow on to the patterned walls. The bed is empty.

The floor still strewn with clothes and discarded plates.

I know she's not here, but I still say, 'Mum?' into the emptiness. There's no reply.

I turn and walk back to my bedroom, mine and Rob's, the room with the holes in the door. The thought of walking back in there makes me feel a bit sick. What if someone's in there, waiting for me? But the light from the landing shows me that there's nothing, just the two mattresses – two crumpled sleeping bags.

In the harsh light of the bare bulb overhead, the room looks smaller and sadder than ever. I look at my watch. Ten past three. Must be ten past three in the morning. I cross to the window and part the curtains. I'm on top of the shops, looking out across an empty street-lit car park and a stretch of grass beyond, fringed by terraces of houses. There's no one about. I rest my elbows on the windowsill, prop my chin in my hands and stare out. I don't exactly remember this, but there's something comforting about it which makes me feel that I've done this before. Stood here. Stared.

After a while, I open the top light of the window and push it as far as it will go, fixing it open by slotting the metal peg on the frame into one of the holes in the handle. It's a still night, but the opening brings some fresh air into the room, and a sort of background hush, nothing you can put your finger on, just the sound a small town makes in its sleep.

No chance of sleep for me. I'm a hundred per cent awake.

I start sifting through some of the stuff on the floor.

T-shirts, socks, pants. There doesn't seem to be a dividing line anywhere, nothing to show what's mine and what's his. Was his, I should say. And there's nothing to say what's clean and what isn't, either. I'm guessing none of it is.

There are food cartons, empty cans of Coke and sweet wrappers all mixed in with the clothes. It's like a sort of soup. I start to separate everything out. Socks in one heap, T-shirts in another. Cans lined up, shoulder to shoulder. I don't even know why I'm doing it, but it's something to do. Patches of floor start to appear. There's carpet under all this, don't know what colour it started off, but it's a sort of grey now, with flecks of brown.

I put actual rubbish in an old plastic bag; cellophane, paper, bits of gum if I can get them off whatever they're stuck on. Soon I've cleared about half the gap between our beds. I pick up another little bit of paper, something torn up. I've already found some of these, put them in my bag, but now I notice that it's not just a bit of a magazine. It's too thick for that, the surface is smooth, shiny. It's a photo. One side's white, but the other has part of a picture. I place it in the palm of my hand and turn it round. There's half a mouth, a chin, shadow at the top of a neck.

I dig about in the rubbish bag and fish out a couple more pieces. I put the three I've got on the floor and slide them about, playing with them, trying to make them fit. And two of them do. Now an eye and half a nose sit above the mouth. It's a girl. I've got a feeling I've seen her before.

I start scrabbling around for the other pieces. I tip the bag out but there aren't any more. I leave the rubbish where it is and turn to sifting through the rest of the stuff on the floor. I'm not sorting it now, just working my way through, picking things from one heap and throwing them behind me into another. Each bit of picture is like a prize. Another piece of a puzzle I've got to solve. I find two more. There's a silver chain round her neck, the top of a T-shirt. She's got two little rings in her right ear, one above the other. I'm missing her left side, though. I keep searching.

The bits are scattered all over the room. I find all of them except two, but I reckon they're both edge bits, so maybe they don't really matter. After a bit of trial and error I've put her face together. She's a striking girl; long, straight dark hair, parted in the middle and tucked behind her ears, smooth skin – no lumps and bumps like me – and beautiful eyes. Deep brown. Dancing with light. You can't help looking at them. She's pouting, pulling her cheeks in, looking up at the camera. I reckon it's one of those pictures you take yourself, you know, with your arm stretched out in front.

There's writing on it, too. She's signed it across the bottom, although that's one of the bits that's missing, so all I can see is, 'Kisses, N—'

Kisses.

The photo is in our room, mine and Rob's. So who was she sending kisses to?

I look round the room, and I think of what I know about my life, my journey here yesterday, standing in the kitchen watching Mum pour lager down her neck, and then I go back to the photo and I look into the girl's eyes again, and I so, so want it to be me those kisses were meant for.

But it can't be. Because the last time I saw her, she screamed at me.

She's the girl in the ambulance.

FOUR

The girl in the photograph. The girl in the ambulance. I need to find out who she is. I need to talk to her. Mum'll know; but where is she, if she isn't in her bed? I leave the pieced-together photo on the floor and start to head downstairs. I've got my foot on the second step when I hear the tap again.

Plip, plip, plip.

I could have sworn I'd turned it off. The washer must be knackered or something.

I turn round and go back into the bathroom. Sure enough, it's the cold tap at the sink again. I twist it firmly and tighten it up. Involuntarily, my shoulders hunch and a shiver runs from the top of my neck to the bottom of my spine. At the same time there's a loud bang from the hallway, a door slamming shut. My heart stops. I duck out on to the landing and it's my room, my door.

My heart's going again now, hard and fast. I can feel my pulse throbbing in my neck. I take a couple of breaths, trying to calm myself down before I tiptoe up to the door, take hold of the handle and turn it slowly and gently. I ease the door open, peering into the room, and finally edge in, checking carefully behind the door. It's empty, of course. The only difference is that the photo isn't on the carpet any more, at least not all in one place. There are bits on my sleeping bag and on Rob's and all over the room. Just like someone picked them up and threw them towards the ceiling. Weird.

I put my hand out of the window. There isn't a breath of wind. I knock the arm off the catch and close it, then I bend down to start picking up the pieces. I could stick them back together with some tape, if we've got any. I keep the pieces in my hand and go downstairs, looking for Mum or some sticky tape, or both.

The lights are all on and Mum's still on the sofa. The sound of the door slamming hasn't bothered her. She's crashed out, the hand with its damaged finger flopping towards the floor like it's pointing at the can that she's dropped. She's well away.

Seeing her like that brings another memory.

'This is how Dad did it.' The blade of Rob's knife is digging into my skin, into the crease that marks the last joint of my little finger. His eyes are cold, hard. The wrong word from me now and he'll cut me.

'Okay, I believe you.'

'Except it was quick, real quick. He got her hand and then brought the knife down, just like this …'

26

I shudder at the thought of Rob pinning my hand down, shudder at what Mum went through, all those years ago. The memories held within these walls are as poisonous as the air. No wonder Mum blots it out with lager.

I hover in the doorway, wondering what the hell I'm going to do now. I don't feel comfortable poking around looking for tape, don't want to disturb her.

There are family photos on top of the telly. I tiptoe past Mum and examine them. Three portraits in cardboard frames, the same two boys in each one. They make a series, tell a story: my brother and me, growing up. Our life in three snapshots. Infant, junior, senior. Tots, boys, teenagers.

If we were in a crowd of a thousand people, a million, you'd pick us out as brothers. Same scruffy hair, same narrow grey-blue eyes sloping down at the outside edges, same cheekbones. Brothers, but not twins. Rob's clearly older – he's bigger than me in every photo. And there's a cockiness about him that's missing in me. In one of the pictures, the most recent one, his head is tipped back a little and he's looking down his nose at the camera. Only slightly, but it's enough to say, loud and clear, 'Yeah, I'm Rob. What about it?' But my eyes don't make contact – I'm not looking straight at the camera, but a little bit to the side.

Now I think of the other photo, the one in pieces in my hand. If you added this girl to one of the photos of me and Rob, where would she go? Next to Rob? Next to me? In front? In between? Where does she fit in?

Behind me, Mum snorts in her sleep. I turn round. She shifts a little, moving on to her back, and then her mouth falls open again and she starts snoring loud enough to rattle the windows.

She's so asleep and I'm so awake. I can't stay here and listen to this, but I don't want to go back upstairs and mess about with taps and doors all night, freaking myself out about people who aren't there.

I stuff the bits of photo into one of the pockets in my jeans and head for the front door. I grab a jacket from the pegs in the hall. Mine or his? Whatever. I put it on. As an afterthought I take another coat, tiptoe back and lay it over Mum. Then I tiptoe to the door, reach for the catch and ease it open.

More flowers have appeared in our yard, leaning up against the door. They flop on to the doormat as I open it. I move them into the hall and leave them there, pulling the door closed behind me.

All these flowers. People must have loved him, mustn't they? He must have been loved. Or are the flowers really for Mum ... sympathy for a woman who's lost a son? I can't help thinking about the fist holes in our bedroom door, remembering the cold look in his eyes as he held the knife to me. Did he keep all that – his violence, his hatred – inside the house? Keep it for Mum and me?

I walk across the yard and on to the concrete walkway, stopping to look over the edge. Garages and more flats beyond, everything soft and quiet, a yellow-orange world. There's a sweet edge to the air as I breathe in, a hint of chocolate. The night shift at the factory must be busy. I look up, trying to see beyond the streetlight halos to the sky beyond. I can't see any stars.

At the top of the stairs I hesitate, then launch myself down, a flying leap taking in four steps at a time – one, two, and then I lean to the side, my hands grab the concrete wall, I flick my legs up and I'm over. It's a two-metre drop the other side. I come crashing down, buckling at the knees. My palms slam into the tarmac and I crouch there for a couple of seconds, working out if I'm okay or not. As I get to my feet, I register a pain in my left ankle and another in my left knee. My leg must have twisted as I fell.

I look round, hoping no one witnessed my landing. Looks like I got away with it. I dust my hands down on the top of my legs, wincing as scuffed-up points of flesh meet denim. Shit!

Glancing back at the stairs, I wonder how Rob made it look so easy, and I see him again in my mind's eye. *He sails over the wall, lands as light as a cat and dances round the girl.*

'Hey, Neisha,' he says. 'What's up?'

He catches hold of her hand and pulls her towards him. And she laughs and her long hair flares outwards as they twirl round in the car park, in tune with each other, moving to the rhythm in their heads. A soundtrack I can't hear.

Neisha.

The girl's name is Neisha.

I turn the corner and strike out across the car park. Maybe being out and about will spark more memories. I know it's all in there. In me. The doctor told me it's just like drawers on a cabinet you can't open, the harder you pull the more they stick. But they're sliding out, slowly. Haven't I just remembered a name that I had no idea about a few minutes ago?

None of this looks familiar, but I'll just walk for a while and follow the same way back.

There's a big open grassy space in front of me. A recreation ground. The only lights are the ones marking out the path that cuts across it. The grass either side glistens in the circles of light they throw out; the rest is in darkness. Goalposts appear like ghosts in the gloom. A kids' play area stands empty inside a knee-high metal fence. The air is thick – not wet exactly, not wet enough to be fog, but not dry either, and now I twig that the reason I can't see the stars is that there's a thick layer of low cloud above me.

I turn my collar up, put my hands in my pockets and hunch my shoulders, trying to protect myself from the cold wet air. I follow the path to the other side of the rec where it dives between back garden fences forming a narrow alleyway. It's darker here. I can't see what I'm treading on, but I keep going, trusting that my feet will find something solid, that there'll be some light soon, that this leads somewhere.

Soon enough it opens up and now I'm in a little estate of bungalows. They're square, neat and tiny. There are ramps up to the doors and tubs of flowers outside. The whole place looks artificial, like it's made of Lego or something.

The estate leads directly into the high street. I recognise it from the trip home in the car, but it's a different place at three-thirty in the morning. Half the shops have their eyes closed – shutters down and locked. The bins are overflowing. Chip wrappers, bottles, flyers and old newspapers. A piece of soggy paper sticks to my shoe. I kick it off, but my eye's caught by a newspaper nearby.

It's a local paper, and I'm on the front page.

It's the photo with Rob looking down his nose, and me not quite looking at the lens. And next to it, a photo of Neisha, not the one I've got in my pocket. This is another school one. Hair brushed. No earrings. White shirt, burgundy tie and cardigan.

I crouch down and read the article, holding the paper up so that it catches the streetlight.

Police are describing the death of local teenager, Robert 'Rob' Adams, 17, as a tragic accident. Robert died on Tuesday after emergency services were called to the lake in Imperial Park, Kingsleigh, at around 4.30pm. Police divers recovered his body from the water, and he was declared dead at the scene.

It is understood that he had been swimming with his brother, Carl, 15, and a friend, Neisha Gupta, 16. Weather conditions were said to be 'atrocious' with Kingsleigh hit by a severe storm at around the same time.

Inspector Dave Anthony of Kingsleigh police said, 'Initial investigations all point to this being a tragic accident. This is a well-known spot where local youngsters often swim in the lake, despite warning signs, and unfortunately it appears that young Rob got into trouble which resulted in his death. We will be talking to the other young people involved when they are up to it, to find out exactly what happened. Our thoughts are with his family and friends.

Sources confirm that a post-mortem has taken place. The results will be reported to the coroner.

Kerry Adams, 34, Robert's mother, was too distraught to comment at the time this went to press.

I read it again, more slowly this time, trying to take in every word. At first reading it just seemed to confirm what I already knew – my brother drowned in a lake. This time, I see that there's more there, much more. Neisha is Neisha Gupta. She's sixteen. There was a storm. The police want to talk to me. There's been a post-mortem. The press have tried to talk to Mum.

I try to process all this. For some reason my mind keeps sticking on the words 'post-mortem'. God, they've cut him up. I don't want to think about it, but I can't stop. Somewhere out there is my brother's body. *The zip goes past his face, over his head.* They've cut into it, looked inside. I glance back at the photo, and I can't get the two things to fit together. A schoolboy, bit cocky, bit tough – and a cut-up body on a slab. Shit.

A drop of water lands in the middle of the photo. I look up and I feel a splash on my face, just to the right of my eye. Cold and light. Another splash hits the paper, and another. It's starting to rain.

It's pounding the surface, bouncing up, making a layer of spray. The lake looks like it's boiling. I can't see the bank any more. I can't see anything, anyone. The rain's pushing me down, the water's pulling at me. Rob and Neisha have disappeared. I can't see them and I can't hear them. I'm treading water, turning my head to left and right, trying to make out anything I can through this relentless wall of rain. Every time I breathe I get water in my mouth. It catches in my throat. I spit and inhale again, and it's the same.

I don't want to be in the rain. I don't want to get wet. My panic is physical. I've got a lump in the back of my throat and my heart's beating fast. I'm sweating and my legs are shaking. I've got to get out of this. I've got to find somewhere to hide.

I pick the newspaper up and stuff it inside my jacket. Then I start running. The rain's coming down heavily. Ahead of me someone darts into a shop doorway. Someone else on the high street, in the middle of the night. I'm almost there – a big ledge overhanging the double doorway to a discount shop. All of a sudden I'm not sure if I want to put myself in that space with a stranger, but the rain pounding on my head persuades me. *Water in my eyes, my nose, my mouth. Water forcing its way down my throat.* I've got to get dry.

I duck into the doorway. It's empty. They must have gone into the shop, but there are no lights on inside, I can't see any movement. I give a little shudder. Something's not right. My face and hair and hands are wet. I'm starting to get cold.

I look out at the high street. It's pouring now, noisy as the rain hits the road and dances up. I close my eyes and somehow I know that I used to like this sound, pattering on the window when I was safe and sound inside. Now it's ringing alarm bells inside my head, it's plucking at my stomach with nervous, busy fingers. A drop of water trickles down the side of my face from my hair.

You bastard, Cee.

The voice is close and threatening. Next to me, whispering in my ear. I open my eyes and look round. Who said that? Who's here?

I'm on my own, an empty street in front of me, solid glass and a dark shop behind. I give another shudder. I'm freaking out. Seeing things, hearing things, things that aren't there. The rain's showing no sign of easing off, but I make the decision to go for it, run through it and home. It's not far.

I turn my collar up and set off, sprinting down the pavement. The rain's starting to make little rivers in the gutters. There's water running down the back of my neck, between my shoulders. My feet slap on the pavement, smacking into the puddling water. Behind me I hear footsteps. I glance behind, but there's no one there. The high street is mine, just me and the rain. So, it must be me I'm hearing. The sound of my own feet echoing off the buildings either side.

The water hits my face and the top of my head. It drips and trickles and dribbles down. It feels like something's alive in between me and my clothes. Something's crawling on my skin. I let out a yell.

There's a flash of light and I can see the whole high street in a split second of unnatural brightness. A few seconds later the deep rumble of thunder starts up.

I skid round the corner by the bungalows, missing my footing and sliding on to the grass. My foot splays out at an angle and I fall awkwardly, wrenching the knee I hurt earlier, cursing as I go down. I put out my hands to stop myself and they slip forward in mud until I'm face down in it. And I can smell it, wet mud in my nostrils and the rain battering on the back of my head. *It's happening again. I'm drowning.*

I turn my head and see Rob's face; white, lifeless, streaked with mud. And the zip moving up and over it.

I scramble to my feet. He's not there, of course. No one else is around, no one else is stupid enough to get caught in a rainstorm in the middle of the night. I could be home in five minutes, but it's lashing down now. The thunder is overhead, ear-splitting explosions like the sky's cracking open.

I duck under the porch of the nearest bungalow, leaning against the blue-painted door. I go to wipe my face with my hands, but my palms are caked with mud. I rub them on my jeans instead and then stuff them in the pockets of the jacket, hoping for a hankie or some tissues. The pockets are deep. My fingers find a crumpled tissue. It's been used and I hesitate for a moment – my snot or his? Does it even matter? I make the best job I can of cleaning myself up with it. Then my hands dive back, because there aren't just tissues in there.

I pull out a packet of fags and a lighter. *Two boys by the lake. Drinking and smoking. Laughing in the sunshine. Me and Rob.*

My hands are shaking as I take a cigarette out. I can hardly hold the lighter still enough to get the fag to catch. I draw the smoke into me. It snags in my throat, just like the water did before, and suddenly I'm struggling for breath again, coughing, choking, bending forward to try and spit my airways clear. Still leaning forward, I drop the cigarette and grind it into the ground. Two boys by the lake, I think wryly. Only one of them smoking and it wasn't me.

So this is Rob's packet of fags. His jacket.

I feel inside again and this time I draw out a phone. It's a cheap-looking touchscreen. I turn it over in my hand, press one of the buttons at the end, and the screen flares into life.

I feel guilty. A guilty thrill. Phones hold names, numbers, messages, pictures. Phones hold people's lives.

I scroll through the address book. There aren't many names, a dozen, no more than that. Neisha Gupta is one of them.

Next, texts: Inbox and Sent. The most recent messages are at the top of the screen.

Sent to Neisha Gupta, 13.29: *Will u b there? 3.30*

Inbox from Neisha Gupta, 13.32: *I said so, dint I?*

I look up, switching my focus from the bright square in my hands to the dark, wet world beyond the porch. Before my eyes properly adjust I think I glimpse a pale figure in the rain – maybe fifteen or twenty metres away from me. I screw my eyes up and look harder, but it's gone.

He knows I've got his phone, I think. But that's nuts. He's dead. Rob's dead.

The screen's gone on to standby, a faint image of itself, hardly there. I press the 'on' button to bring it back, and look through the menu.

Gallery: the first picture is a bit like the one I've got torn up in my pocket. Neisha, pouting for the camera. It's more vivid on the screen than on paper, more real. My stomach flips as I look into her eyes again. She's beautiful. Sexy. But now I can't have any doubt – she was looking into this lens, this phone, when that photo was taken. She was looking at Rob.

Neisha Gupta. Rob's girl.

I drag my finger across the screen to find the next picture. It's not just her face this time. It's a wider shot, taken in a bedroom, not ours. She's in her knickers and bra, sitting on the bed, leaning forward towards the camera. One of the straps is hanging off her shoulder. She's not pouting any more, but she's not smiling either. Her expression is uncertain, like she doesn't know what to do with her face. But it's not her face I'm looking at.

My fingers are sweaty as I scroll to the next shot. She's smiling now but only with the edges of her mouth, the rest of her face is scared. Her left cheekbone is redder than the other one and I can't help reliving what it felt like when Mum slapped me in the taxi. Her eyes are pleading with the camera. Pleading for what? I feel dirty looking at her, but I don't, *can't*, stop looking. My eyes drink in her soft curves, the warm honey tones of her skin. She's still wearing her necklace. A heart-shaped locket dangles at the end of the silver chain, resting dead centre between her naked breasts.

'*Just give me your necklace and I'll go.*'

Rob's voice is in my head, a memory's forming that I can't quite get hold of. He wasn't talking to Neisha. Who was it?

I hear a noise behind me. I jab at the 'off' button, and quickly stuff the phone back in my pocket. A light's come on in the bungalow behind me. Shit!

The rain's eased off a little. I turn the collar up further on my jacket and make a run for it. My head is full of the hot guilt of seeing the pictures on the phone. It's only when I'm halfway across the rec that I think about the light, the rows of bungalows facing each other around a scrubby grass square, and it triggers another memory.

Rob's in front of me in a dark house; I can hear barking. Then there's a yelp and the barking stops. Rob's heading into the front room ... I can see something on the floor between me and him, a mound, a still, dog-shaped heap.

'What is it, Winston?' A woman's voice, old, quavering.

'Rob, get out! Get out now!' I hiss.

And then a light flicks on.

I've stopped walking. I'm standing in the middle of the rec. The play area for the little kids is to my right. There's an ugly pod of parallel metal bars, which offers no shelter from anything at all, to my left.

In a daze, I walk over to the metal shell and perch on the bars. They are spotted with rain and I can feel it soaking through, adding to the wetness already there. The rain's gently pattering on the ground around me but I'm not hearing it. I'm hearing a yelping dog, then a moment of silence and the old lady's voice, pleading with Rob. Cursing him. I hear my voice, too. Scared. Panicking.

I feel churned up inside, sick. The brick wall in my head, the blankness, was better than this. Maybe there was a reason I forgot everything. Maybe this was the reason. The truth is best forgotten.

There's no vibration through the metal, there's no

noise, but suddenly I know I'm not on my own any more. There's someone close. I sense him and shudder, thinking of the shadow darting into the doorway, the pale shape across the street.

I force myself to twist round and look through the metal bars. I jump. There's a face looking back. The eyes are fixed on mine. The lips move.

You bastard, Cee.

I blink and he's gone.

Shit! I've got to get out of here. Go home. I'm going mad. My mind is playing tricks.

I jump up from my perch and stumble across the rec, looking all around me as I run. I go round the back of the parade and haul myself up the steps. There's a set of keys in the other pocket. I let myself in and head straight upstairs. I don't check the room first. I just go in, drop the jacket on the floor, strip off my wet things, towel my hair with a dry T-shirt from the heap and flop down on my mattress. I lie on my right side, facing the wall, so I can't see Rob's sleeping bag, and I close my eyes tight shut.

This time I don't hear him breathing as I drift off, and I don't hear him telling me to say goodnight, but at the last moment something clicks in my brain and just before I'm away, I whisper the words, 'Night, Rob.' And that's the last thing I hear, my own voice ... and the drip, drip, drip of the bathroom tap.

FIVE

I have restless dreams, dreams where I don't know if I'm awake or asleep, what's real and what isn't. Dreams of me, of Rob, of Neisha. With her clothes on. With her clothes off. When I finally wake up, the first thought that hits me is, My brother's dead. Rob's dead.

I'm in our room, on my own, and he's dead. The words are starting to mean something now. He was dead yesterday and he's still dead today. Is it always going to be like this? This sledgehammer? Is this how I'll wake up for the rest of my life?

It's light. I stick my hand out from the clammy folds of my sleeping bag, grope around the floor by my bed until I find my watch. It says ten past three. I shake my head and look again. The second hand's ticking round, so it's working. It must be the afternoon.

I leave the sleeping bag in a heap on my mattress. Where the curtains are parted I can see condensation fogging up the window, blotting out the world outside. I stagger into the bathroom, trying not to put too much weight on my painful left leg. The cold tap is still dripping; it's even worse now.

Catching my reflection in the mirror, my heart jumps into the back of my throat. The shape of my face, the angle of the grey-blue eyes, the set of my mouth and the lines of dirt. All these things say Rob. The face they zipped away – eyes open, skin pale and streaked with mud.

But I'm not Rob. I've got to remember that. I look like him, but that's all. We were at the lake together, we were there, struggling in the water ... but I got out alive.

The dirt on my face must be from when I fell over by the bungalows. I feel a judder of revulsion, but I can wash it away. I can clean myself up. I reach for the hot tap and wince: my palm is sore. There are little raw points, bright red oozy pinpricks, where the skin's been taken off. I put the plug in and start to turn the tap, but then I stop, remembering what happened last night when I splashed my face.

The memories. The voice.

But it was the middle of the night. I was tired. Confused.

Even so, I check behind me. There's no one there, of course.

I watch the water dripping from the cold tap, forming a clear pool in the bottom of the sink, and anxiety stabs me in the guts.

For Chrissake, just have a wash. Look at you. You're a mess. A voice in my head is urging me on.

I turn the hot tap full on, so it's gushing and spluttering, and dip one hand into the water, swooshing it round to feel the temperature. I'm looking down but my eye catches something flashing in the mirror behind me, a movement. It's gone before I'm even sure if I saw it, but my chest starts heaving, and I can feel sweat prickling on my upper lip. I spin round and face the room.

It's empty.

I turn back to the sink. *Come on, you can do this.* The water is nearly up to the outlet. I turn the hot tap off and tighten up the cold one so that stops dripping too. I plunge both hands into the water, lean forward and splash my face.

She's screaming. Her hands are tearing at his, trying to wrench them away from her throat. I take another deep breath and swim towards them. I look up again. Rain splashes on the surface making it seem alive, obscuring my view. But I can still hear her. Hear her screaming for her life.

There's sweat between my shoulder blades, my stomach's contracting, my heart's pounding. It's not real; it's a memory, that's all. I force myself to pick up the soap and work my hands together. I lean forward again and scrub my cheeks and forehead, along my jaw line and round my eyes.

Get clean, wash all this away.

I slop water on to my face again to rinse it. When I open my eyes the soapy drips have merged with the rest, clouding the water in the bowl below. I can still see the dark circle of the plug at the bottom, but there's something else. A face looking up at me.

His face. Deathly pale. Marked skin.

'No!'

I rear back, fumbling for the towel. I dry my face and inch forward, peering over the rim of the sink. There's a pale shadow there now, the outline of a face and neck. Trembling, I lean closer. The shape gets larger. Closer still. Larger again.

It's me, of course. My reflection on the surface of the water.

I pull the plug and watch the water disappear. Then I look at myself in the mirror.

How can you tell if you're going mad? Do you look different? Can you see it in your own eyes?

SIX

Downstairs, the lounge is a mess, cans lying where Mum left them last night. The coat I put on top of her is on the floor. But she's not there. I check in the kitchen, then go back through to the bottom of the stairs and shout up.

'Mum?'

I run up and knock on the other bedroom door.

'Mum?'

No reply. I look in quickly. The bed's empty, the duvet's half on the floor. There are old tissues and cans littering the carpet. But no Mum. Where the hell is she? I've just got out of hospital and she isn't even here.

I'm really thirsty; hungry too. But there's no food in the place and nothing to drink except lager, water and some off milk. I want something to get me going, get my senses working properly – something with some fizz, some caffeine.

I grab last night's jacket from the floor and clatter down the stairs. I have a quick look for some money. Surely there's some cash lying around somewhere, for God's sake, some emergency notes stashed in a biscuit tin or under a can in the cupboard. I do a quick trawl of the kitchen and lounge, stick my hand down the back of the sofa. I find fifteen pence between the cushions, and that's it. I drop the coins in my jeans pocket.

On my way out of the lounge I put the jacket on and explore the pockets. My fingers close around the phone, and last night's guilty heat surges through me again. Don't look now. Concentrate. As well as the packet of fags and the lighter, there's something smooth, heavy when I close my fingers around it. Without looking, I know it's a jack-knife. I can see it in his hand, as he flicks the blade in and out, in and out. I let it go and keep searching in, digging into the corners of both pockets. No coins. Shit.

I pull the door shut behind me. I need some food, but I've no idea how I'm going to get it. I jog tentatively along the walkway and down the stairs – no vaulting over the edge today. There are some little kids playing football by the garages. They stop when they see me, just stop and stare silently. One of them picks up the ball and holds it close to his chest.

I trot round the corner and swing into the shop on the end of the parade. It's the sort of place that sells every-thing – papers, bog roll, sweets, bread, booze – if you've got any money, which I haven't. Well, hardly any. I'm just hoping I'll think of something.

The guy behind the counter clocks me as soon as I walk in. He holds his hand up to the customer at the till. 'One moment,' he says, then he leans over the desk and calls across the shop to me.

'You're banned. Don't you remember? I don't want any more of my stuff going missing.'

I start to colour up. The people in the queue are looking now. He's as good as called me a thief in front of them.

'I just want to get a few things,' I say, trying to stay calm. I'm thinking that maybe I can ask to owe him or say that my mum will pay him back.

He shakes his head.

'Not in here.'

'Please, I'm hungry and thirsty. We've got nothing in the house. Mum hasn't had a chance to get anything in since ... since, you know.'

The guy's expression softens. Two of the people in the queue look away, the woman nearest the till makes a sympathetic face. They all know.

'Just a can of Coke and some bread or something,' I say.

The guy nods reluctantly. 'Okay. Quickly,' he says.

I open the fridge and pretend to take my time choosing, running my hand across the top of the cans. When the shop guy goes back to serving the woman, I slip a can into the inside pocket of my jacket, and then take another. It's instinctive, my hand does it so quickly. And it was easy, so easy – I must have done it before. I feel bad, but I haven't got any money, have I? If he doesn't let me have the one he can see, at least I'll have the one in my pocket.

I follow the aisle round and pick up some sliced white and a tin of beans, then I walk up to the queue.

'You go in front, love,' the woman close to the till says. 'That's all right, isn't it?' she says to the people behind. They both mutter something that could be 'yeah', too embarrassed to do anything else. I shuffle past them and stand next to her. I still don't know how I'm going to play this.

'Can I owe you?' I say to the guy, nervously.

He looks at me in disbelief.

'What?' he says.

'Can I owe you? Mum's gone out and taken all the cash.'

His hand shoots out and he's gripping the top of the baked bean can. I was an idiot to even try this, but what else was I supposed to do?

'What are you doing, coming into my shop with no money? What are you doing?' His voice is much too loud and a little bit of spit lands on the top of the hand holding the can.

I can hear tutting behind me, but the woman's scrabbling in her purse. She hands me a two-pound coin.

'It's all right, Ashraf,' she says. 'Here, Carl, pay with this.'

Ashraf looks at her like she's completely lost her marbles.

I smile at her gratefully, put the coin on the counter and slide it towards Ashraf.

He blows air out slowly through pursed lips, takes the

47

coin like it's infected with AIDS and puts my change on the counter. I look at the money and then at the woman.

'You have it,' she says. 'Go on, take it. How's your mum doing?'

Violent. Tearful. Drunk. Missing. Tears start welling up. She's being too nice and I'm just not used to it.

'She's okay,' I say. 'She's doing okay.'

'Give her my best,' she says. 'Tell her Sue from the launderette sends her love.'

I nod my head, then pocket the coins and make a swift exit carrying my stuff in a thin plastic bag. I open the Coke outside the shop. It's cold and sweet and fizzy, with that prickly edge to it that you get from the first sip. I neck it thirstily as I walk across to the rec and the bubbles go up my nose, and another memory comes out of the fog in my mind.

I pass her the can and she takes a hearty swig, then hands the can back quickly, laughing and flapping her hand in front of her face.

'You all right?'

'Yeah, went up my nose. That'll teach me to drink so fast.'

I put the can to my lips, slurping at the liquid that's collected just inside the top rim, aware of my lips touching the lip gloss she's left behind.

She stretches her legs out in front of her, leans back into the park bench and puts her hands behind her head. The sun is bright in our faces and she closes her eyes.

'This is nice,' she says.

I don't close my eyes. I sip at the Coke and look at Neisha's face, her beautiful face in the sunshine.

The rec is filling up with kids — little ones in the play

park, bigger ones in uniform hanging round the shelter or swinging on a tyre someone's rigged up in a tree. They stream on to the square of grass and mud from one corner and it takes a minute until the penny drops: they're all coming out of school.

School. Mum hasn't mentioned it and I simply forgot all about it. It doesn't seem, I dunno, important. No one can expect me to sit in lessons and take it all in when my brother's died, can they? I'm fifteen. I can't even remember who my school mates are. If I've got any. Perhaps I'll never have to go to school again.

I lean against a tree and finish my Coke. There's a heavy feeling behind my eyes, a sort of pressure, and I realise I'm not far off crying again.

I look at the ground in front of me and scuff the toe of my trainers in the dirt, then throw my empty Coke can towards the bin. It misses. I leave it lying on the ground, turn away and start walking back to the flat, eyes on the ground.

'Aren't you going to pick that up?'

I look up. Coming towards me is a woman in uniform. She's young, younger than Mum anyway, sturdy-looking with gingerish curly hair which is trying to escape from under her hat.

'I'll get it,' she says. 'This time.' She stoops down, picks up the can and drops it in the bin, then walks over to stand next to me. 'How are you doing, Carl? I'm surprised to see you out. Only got home yesterday, didn't you?'

She seems to know all about me, but I don't know her. At least I don't think I do. I'm suddenly aware of the can in my inside pocket, the fags, the knife, the phone, the photos. Oh God. I fold my arms across my front.

'I'm okay,' I say, avoiding her look.

'I called round earlier but no one answered,' she says. 'We need to talk to you, about Tuesday. I know you talked about it to someone in hospital, but this is important. We need to go over it again. You on your way home now?'

'Yeah, but I'm not sure …' If the house is still empty. Where Mum's gone. If she's ever coming back.

'It's okay, I'll give your mum a ring. See if I can come round. It needs to be today, really. Sooner rather than later.'

She's saying it kindly, but I've got alarm bells going off. What does she want? I've got nothing to tell her. All the stuff I can remember isn't the sort of thing you'd tell a copper.

'Yeah, okay …' I say vaguely and start to wander away.

'I'm sorry about Rob,' she says. I stop and stare at the ground. 'We had our ups and downs, but I was very sorry to hear what happened. It's a terrible shame.'

I kind of nod, and start walking again. Got to get out of here.

'I'll see you later, right?'

'Right, okay,' I say.

I start running towards the flat, but have to stop. I feel almost sick, unpleasantly full. Running and Coke don't mix.

The flat's still empty. I take a few deep breaths like they showed me at the hospital, try to put everything out of my mind – Mum, Rob, the police, Neisha. God, Neisha. I'm itching to get the phone out, look at the photos again, but my stomach starts rumbling and I realise I can't remember the last time I ate something. I think about that rather than the growing panic inside me, and set about cooking up a storm. I put a couple of slices of bread in the toaster and press the lever down, but nothing happens. It just pops up again. There's no heat or anything. Okay, I'll do it under the grill. It's all electric so all I have to do is find the right knob and turn it on. How frickin' hard can it be? I get the grill going – four slices lined up now, nice and neat – and turn my attention to the beans. I fetch a pan out of the cupboard, slam it on the cooker top, turn on the ring and empty one of the tins into it.

I wander into the lounge and flick the TV on to keep my mind off the policewoman. It's some sort of cooking programme. I watch as the guy on screen chops up a load of veg and then starts to fry it. He's already got some meat sizzling in the pan. He's stirring it round, adding more stuff, squirting some sort of sauce on it – to be honest, it looks pretty tasty. I can't take my eyes away. I can almost smell it and the pain in my stomach is really going for it now, stabbing me from the inside. He tips the food on to a big square white plate and bends over to smell his creation.

I breathe in with him, expecting meat and onion and I don't know what else. I get smoke, bitter and choking in the back of my throat. Shit! I jump back into the kitchen. Grey smoke is streaming up and out of the grill. I grab the grill pan. It burns my fingers as I yank it clear and let it drop on to the floor, on to the heap of wilting flowers. Their plastic wrappings hiss and shrivel in the heat. The toast is black and the beans in the saucepan have almost disappeared. What's wrong with me? I just wanted some food. I'm so bloody hungry. The tears that were threatening to burst out earlier are back.

Why isn't Mum here to do this? Why didn't she teach me what to do? Where the hell is she?

I stand in the middle of the kitchen, hands hanging by my sides, crying like a baby.

'Carl?'

She's there, in the doorway, looking at the mayhem.

'What's going on here? Do you mind telling me what the hell is going on?'

SEVEN

'I was hungry, Mum. There was no food and you weren't here. What am I supposed to do?' My voice goes higher as I rant on. 'Where were you? Where *were* you, Mum?'

She says nothing, does nothing. She's just standing there and now I notice that she's got a bag of shopping in each hand, blue and white Tesco bags bulging full of stuff. Her face looks thinner than ever, the creases deeper. Her hair's lank and greasy. She's tied it back, but some of it has escaped. She's thirty-four but she looks about fifty.

'Where've you been?' I ask again. My throat is sore from shouting.

'I went to see about the funeral,' she says.

It feels like the bottom's dropping out of my world. The funeral. I'd forgotten there'd have to be a funeral.

I step over the grill pan, avoiding the plastic flower

wrappers, take her shopping bags and put them on the table. On the hob the saucepan's still making a horrible noise. I switch off the ring and the grill and open a window.

Mum just stands there, looking lost in her own kitchen.

'Do you want to sit down?' I say. She stumbles to the kitchen table and lowers herself slowly on to a chair. 'Do you want a drink?'

She nods and I grab the kettle. I turn towards the sink and stop, suddenly nervous about turning on the tap. It's stupid, but I can't help it.

'No,' Mum says, 'a real drink.' She flips her fingers towards the fridge. Breathing out, I set the kettle back on the worktop, reach into the fridge for a can and put it on the table in front of her. She cradles it with both hands, but she doesn't do anything else. I lean across and crack it open.

'Ta,' she says, and takes a sip. 'I got lots of leaflets and stuff,' she says. 'Have a look.' She digs in her handbag and hands me a heap of papers. *When a Child Dies. Bereavement Benefits. Guide to Hayfield Cemetery. Children and Funerals.*

I start reading one, but it just makes me feel sick. I push it away, across the table.

'Have you decided what's gonna happen, then?'

She knows what I'm asking, but she doesn't answer straight away. She purses her lips and sucks on the inside of her mouth. I think she's going to cry, but she doesn't. After a while she says, 'He'll be cremated and then we'll have the ashes here. It doesn't seem right to have them buried or anything. We'll bring him home.'

'Cremated?' Burnt up. That can't be right. It's so … so final.

'Yeah. Is that all right with you? I didn't know what to do, Carl. I had to make a decision. But we could change it, if you're not happy.'

'Happy.' The word sits like ash in my mouth.

'I don't mean happy,' she says quickly. 'I didn't mean that. I didn't mean …' Her eyes are filling up now.

'It's all right,' I say, trying to stop it before it starts. 'It's all right. What you said, it's okay. We'll do that.'

'Okay,' she says. 'It's next Tuesday. The funeral.'

Her hand's resting on the leaflet. She's stroking the paper gently.

'You wouldn't believe how much this all costs. The funeral lady said Rob's half price because he's only seventeen, *was* only seventeen … It's free if you're under five.'

There's nowhere to go with that. I let it hang in the air for a bit. It's still hanging when a phone starts ringing. Mum looks panicked.

'It's yours, Mum,' I say. 'Is it in your bag?'

'Who is it?' she says, as if I would know.

'It's your phone, Mum.'

'You get it. I … I can't.'

She reaches into her bag and hands the phone to me. Caller Unknown. I press the green button and answer.

It's the policewoman I saw earlier. My guts turn to jelly.

Her name's PC Sally Underwood. She asks to talk to Mum, but Mum just shakes her head.

'I'm sorry, she can't come to the phone right now.'

'But she's there? She's at home?'

'Yeah.'

'Is it all right if I call round with a colleague in about a quarter of an hour?'

'Yeah,' I say, even though I don't want her to come and I don't know if it's all right with Mum. I've just got a gut feeling that saying no would make everything worse.

She rings off.

'Who was it?' Mum asks.

'The Old Bill.'

I can see her jawbone through her skin as she clenches her teeth.

'They want to come round in a few minutes. Interview me. I saw one of them earlier.'

She looks down at the table. She's crumpling the bereavement leaflet in her hand, but I don't think she even knows she's doing it.

'What's wrong, Mum? Why wouldn't you answer your phone?'

'That's how they told me,' she says quietly. 'The police called and told me that Rob was … in trouble. I was still on the phone when someone ran into the pub and said he was dead. And you were on your way to hospital.'

'I'm sorry. I'm sorry, Mum.' I'm doing it now – saying sorry for things that aren't my fault, like the policewoman did.

Fifteen minutes. She's coming here in fifteen minutes. I look at the floor – the grill pan, the bits of black toast, flowers and plastic. I think of the cans scattered around the sofa. I can't let her see the place like this.

'Look,' I say, 'she'll be here soon. Let's tidy up a bit.'

I pick the grill pan off the floor and slide it back into its slot. I put the burnt toast in the bin and start scooping up the flowers.

'Mum, why don't you pick up the cans in the lounge, and I'll do the floor in here? What do I use?'

'Under the sink,' she says, but makes no sign of moving from her chair.

In the cupboard under the sink there's a plastic bucket, with a cloth draped over the side and a bottle of Flash.

I stand the bucket in the sink and squirt some cleaner into it. Then I turn on both taps. Water thunders in. A layer of foam forms, rising up the inside of the bucket. Fear starts rising up in me at the sight of it. God, it's only water. Get a grip!

I dart into the lounge and pick up the empty cans. When I get back the bucket's nearly full. I dump the cans in the bin and turn off the tap. Mum's still sitting at the table.

'Mum, please …'

She watches as I haul the bucket on to the floor. I dip the cloth into the soapy water. It's icy cold. I wring the cloth out and a scream rips through my head. It's so loud it's painful, like someone poking a knitting needle into one ear and out the other.

I jerk my head up. The screaming's stopped but I'm confused, disorientated.

I move the bucket forward and water sloshes over the top. A puddle spreads out from its base. I tip forward, stretching to mop it up, and I've suddenly got a feeling of pressure in my throat. I swallow hard but something comes up inside and now my mouth is full of cold, rank liquid. I clamber on to my feet and spit into the kitchen sink. As the stuff leaves my mouth I get a whiff of something stale, something stagnant and muddy and slimy.

'Jesus!' I splutter. I'm gasping for air.

'What—?' Mum's finally on her feet. She stares at the puddle gathering around the plughole – brown fluid streaked with mucus – then she turns on the tap to flush it away. 'Rinse your mouth out,' she says. Her words are harsh, but she puts her hand between my shoulder blades and moves it up and down gently and I remember other times like this. Head held over the toilet, puking my guts up, and a reassuring hand on my back. Rob's, not hers.

I hang my head under the tap, sucking the clean water in, puffing out my cheeks and swishing it from one side of my mouth to the other before I spit.

I'm coming for you, Cee. It's the voice, the one I heard before. It's right beside me.

I straighten up.

'Did you hear that?' I say to Mum.

'What?'

'That voice.'

She looks blank.

'I can't hear anything except the tap running and you spitting. Are you done now?'

There's still an echo of the staleness in my mouth, lurking in the little gaps at the base of my teeth.

'Nearly.'

I dunk my head under again.

58

Can you hear me, little brother?

I look at the water cascading out of the tap end towards my face, and I get a glimpse of something. A stillness in the middle of the rushing water. It's so close but I can't make it out. It makes me uneasy, but at the same time it draws me to it.

The doorbell rings, snapping me out of it. I stand up and switch off the tap. Mum seems paralysed, eyes full of uncertainty.

'I'll go,' I say, wiping my face on a tea-towel as I walk through into the hall.

The interview isn't a success. My memory is so hazy and nothing in my head makes sense. I can't answer even the easy questions.

'Why were you at the lake?'

'I dunno.'

'What did you do before you went to the lake? Tell me about that day.'

'I can't remember.'

'What happened when you were in the water?'

'I dunno. I just remember it raining, chucking it down, and there was thunder and lightning.'

'When the emergency services found you, you had your school trousers on and your shirt, but Rob only had his underpants on. Why were you swimming in your clothes, Carl?'

'I dunno. I'm sorry. I really don't remember.'

'Carl, I need to ask you this. There were bruises and scratches on Rob's ... on him. Do you know how they came to get there?'

My knuckles connect with the side of his head. He recoils and comes back at me. I'm punching and kicking, but the water's making my arms and legs slow and heavy and I'm cold, so cold. It's draining the power out of me. I flex my feet trying to kick him with my heels and I do, I get him. He's shouting and screaming. And he's giving as good as he gets.

'No, I dunno.' I can feel my palms starting to sweat. If these memories are real, then it was me who made the scratches and bruises.

Mum's sitting on the edge of her seat. Her hands are clasped together between her legs, back rounded, shoulders hunched. She looks like she's in a dentist's waiting room or something, not sitting in her own front room.

'Boys are always fighting, aren't they?' she says now. 'That's what boys do.'

PC Underwood frowns, but it's the other one that leans forward in his chair and asks, 'When did you last see them fighting, Kerry?'

God, what's he getting at? Does he think I had something to do with it? Does he know?

Mum looks down at her hands.

'They were always at it,' she says. 'I don't know.'

'Were they fighting at home? In the morning? Earlier in the afternoon?'

'I don't know. I slept in that morning. And when I got up ...'

'When you got up?'

There's a pause. He definitely thinks he's on to something.

'… I went to the pub.'

Mum retreats back into her shell, head down, shoulders near her ears. I try to stay calm.

The male copper makes some notes in his book. PC Underwood glances at a can under the coffee table, one I must have missed when I was gathering them all up. Damn. I hate this, people like them, coming here. Looking. Judging.

Underwood turns back to me.

'Can you remember anything else at all, Carl?'

'There was a girl there,' I say.

'Neisha Gupta,' she says.

'Rob's girlfriend,' Mum murmurs. 'God, I forgot about her.'

His girlfriend.

Pouting for the camera lens. The strap falling away from her shoulder. Stop it. For God's sake, stop!

'We've interviewed her already. She's … she's very shaken up.'

'I bet she is, poor love. What did she say? What happened?'

'She didn't want to talk about it. It's obviously very painful for her. But she did say that the three of them were swimming, larking about, and they were fine until the weather turned. Then it was raining so much they couldn't see, they got separated and when she and Carl found each other, they realised Rob wasn't with them.'

'*We were fine until the weather turned … larking about …*' She's lying. I was hitting him, wasn't I? Why has she lied to the police?

Mum swallows hard. I can see she's trying not to cry.

'Do you remember that, Carl?' Mum says to me. 'Do you remember any of it?'

'I remember the rain, that's all.' There's no way I'm gonna say anything else until I clearly remember what happened, the whole picture.

'You should talk with her. It might help,' Underwood says.

She and her mate get ready to leave. Mum asks what happens next, and she says that there'll be an inquest, an inquiry into how he died. The coroner, who's in charge of it all, has released Rob's body to the undertaker, so the funeral can go ahead, and then the inquest will be a little while after that. She fixes me with a look, as if she knows I'm not telling her everything, and asks me to get in touch with her if I remember any more, then they're gone.

As the door closes behind them, I suddenly feel very tired. Mum sits back on the sofa, closes her eyes and lets out a big sigh. I try doing the same. I've got a powerful feeling of needing to sleep, like the chair's dragging on my arms and legs, making them heavy. But when I close my eyes I see the face in the sink, staring up at me. I hear the voice again: I'm coming, Cee.

I open my eyes and sit bolt upright. I've got to tell someone what I remember. Get it off my chest. It's eating me up.

'Mum, are you awake?'

She stirs a little and her eyes flicker open.

'Just about,' she says.

'Mum, I do remember more.'

She opens her eyes properly now, leans forward.

'You do?'

'Yeah, not much. But we were fighting. In the lake. Me and Rob, we were fighting.'

She frowns.

'What were you fighting about?'

'I dunno. I can't remember that.'

She lets out another big sigh and rolls her eyes up to the ceiling.

'Always fighting. I don't know how many times I had to tell you two.'

'Mum, what if I ... what if I ...' I can't say it. 'Mum, what if ...?'

She knows what I'm trying to get out, and she doesn't want to hear it any more than I want to say it. She holds her index finger up to her lips.

'Don't,' she says. 'Don't. It was an accident. That's what it was. An accident.'

'I can hear him, Mum. I can see him.'

I'm almost certain. It doesn't make sense, but it's true. It's true. The figure in the rain, the face in the sink and the voice in my head – they're his. Rob's.

She gets up from the sofa and perches on the arm of my chair, putting her arm round my shoulders.

'Of course you can,' she says. 'It's only natural. You've been through a lot, Carl. You're grieving. It's going to take time.'

'Do you see him too?'

'Everywhere,' she says. 'He's everywhere, isn't he? Especially here. I keep expecting him to walk through that door ...'

She sighs and squeezes my shoulder. And I want to believe it's the same for both of us – a normal part of grieving. But from across the hallway, I can hear a noise from the kitchen. The *plip, plip, plip* of a tap dripping on to the metal of the sink. And it makes me feel sick.

EIGHT

In my bedroom, I retrieve Rob's phone from the jacket pocket and dial Neisha's number. We were there, at the lake, all three of us – Rob, Neisha and me. I need to find out what she knows. I need her to fill in the gaps.

After half a dozen rings, someone answers.

'Hello?'

A girl's voice. It's her. Neisha. Somehow I wasn't expecting her to actually answer. I haven't worked out what to say.

'Um ... hello?' I can hardly speak.

'Hello? Hello? Who is this?' she says, her voice shaking.

'Is that Neisha? Neisha Gupta?'

'Yes, this is Neisha. Who is it?'

'It's me. Carl.'

'Carl?'

'I need to talk to you. I need—'

The phone's cut off. She's gone.

I redial. This time it rings for ages, then an answer-phone cuts in.

'Hi, this is Neisha. I can't get to the phone right now, so leave a message after the tone and I'll get right back atcha!' She signs off with a kiss, and now I'm thinking of her lips, pouting, in the photo. I'm thinking about her bare shoulders, her ...

The phone bleeps in my ear and, startled, I start rambling.

'Neisha, it's me, Carl. I really need to talk to you. I've got so many questions. I can't remember properly. I can't remember what happened. You were there. You're the only person who can ...'

There's a fumbling noise and then she's back, cutting across me.

'I've got nothing to say to you. Leave me alone, Carl. Leave me alone!'

And then blank again. Nothing but the sound of my own breathing and the crackle of static.

She doesn't want anything to do with me, that much is obvious. But why? What have I done to her? She sat next to me in the park, relaxed and happy in the sunshine. What happened? What changed?

The suspicion that's been bugging me is turning into something more solid. I remember fighting Rob in the water. I survived. He didn't.

Did I kill him?

Did I kill my brother?

Is that why Neisha hates me? Is that why she's so scared?

But that's not what she told the police. She told them she didn't know how he died, that we were just mucking about. I don't understand.

I've got to see her. If that's what I am — a murderer — I need to know what happened. What made me do something like that.

I fetch the phone book from the front room. My fingers are shaking as I page through. There's only one Gupta with an address in Kingsleigh. 8 River Terrace. I find it on the town map. It's halfway between the estate and the factory, near where the road bridge crosses the river. I fix a route in my head, and as I do so, I can see it, see the paths, and alleys and roads. I've been there before — and now I remember: following Rob, standing in the road, watching the house, the silhouettes in the window … and the burning jealousy smouldering inside me.

'True what they say about these Asian birds, little brother. They know some tricks, they do. Stands to reason. That's where the Karma Sutra came from, isn't it?'

A memory of Neisha's face — her deep brown eyes, her full lips — comes back to me. Suddenly I know there was a time when I couldn't get her out of my mind. She was there as I chugged down the beer, there when I went upstairs, there when I lay on my bed, unzipped and put my hand inside my pants.

The feelings are all here inside me. He pushed me out. He didn't need me any more. And I was jealous of him and he liked it. He taunted me. And I wanted her, and it

67

was never going to happen, because he was there. He was always there. Older, bigger, tougher.

Behind me, the dripping of the tap in the bathroom sets the hairs on the back of my neck standing up.

This is stupid. It's just water, for Chrissake.

I jump up and stride into the bathroom. I wrench the tap round until it won't do up any further.

'Just stop it, okay? Stop it!' I say out loud.

'You all right up there?' Mum calls up from the front room.

'Yeah, yeah, I'm fine. I'm going out.'

I start down the stairs. She's waiting in the hallway.

'Where you going?'

'Out. Some fresh air.'

'Don't go, Carl. It's going to be dark soon.'

She's holding a can in one hand. The other hand is by her mouth and she's gnawing at the edge of her fingernail. The skin's red and sore. She looks up at me, and I realise, with a pang, that she doesn't want to be alone.

'I won't be gone for long, Mum. I just gotta see someone.'

She shrugs.

'I'll be back soon, promise.'

I open the front door, pull my hood over my head and set off down the road, away from the rec. I keep my eyes down, I only need to see far enough ahead to avoid the dog shit and the puddles. The hood muffles the noise of the estate and as I duck into an alleyway, all I can hear is my own breathing and the thudding of my heart.

I don't see the three lads in my path till it's too late. Not till I come face to boozy face with them.

They're older and bigger than I am, wearing new tracksuits and Nikes. Side by side, arms folded, feet planted squarely, blocking the path.

I don't recognise them, but it's obvious they know me … and they don't like me.

The alleyway is narrow with high wooden fences. There's just room for two people to pass without going in the mess of nettles and brambles and rubbish either side. I've got no chance.

I look behind me, but that's my second mistake – I should have piled in with my fists straight away or just run, run back the other way as fast as I could. Now I'm shoved sideways, squashed into a spiky bush. Razor-sharp thorns tear at my clothes and skin, pulling my hood away from my face. The air's been knocked out of me and I'm struggling for breath. Panicking.

One of the guys, an ugly dude with half his hair shaved off, is pushing my chest further back. 'On your own? Ha, ha, dumb question. Hey, at least one of you's dead. Saves us half the trouble.'

I reckon I might be able to knee him in the nuts, take him out, but there are the other two. Three against one is never going to end well.

The rain's started again and another wave of panic breaks over me, my automatic response now to water.

Another shove to my chest and I grunt as my back hits the fence behind. Shaved Head sniffs hard, turning his head left and right.

'There's a nasty smell around here,' he says. 'How many

times do I have to tell you not to pollute my manor, you dickhead? I told you I'd kill you if I saw you here again.' He brings his hand up towards me and I feel something cold against my neck, a sharp edge digging in. Shit, he's got a knife. 'Course, I've got one too, but if I get it out, someone's going to get hurt. This could be a bloodbath. I'm still hoping I can bluff my way out of this.

Behind him, something seems to crystallise in the drizzle. Something pale, shimmering. I'm distracted by it, but I've got to concentrate, play this smart if I'm going to get out of here in one piece.

'Look,' I gasp, 'I don't want any trouble. Just let me go, okay?'

'You should of thought of that before you put your stinking feet on my patch.'

'I'm sorry,' I say. 'My head got bashed in the lake, I only got out of hospital yesterday. I don't even know who you are.'

The rain is getting harder and the thing behind him is taking shape. A face with dark, dark eyes. Black holes, a dark smudge for a mouth. Even though I've got a knife at my neck I can't help staring at it, watching it form.

The face – distorted, blurred, strange – is the face in the school photo, the face on the front page.

Rob. My brother. He's not dead after all. He's here …

'You're not even listening, you little arse-wipe.'

Suddenly, the pressure on my neck is released and I think he's backing off, that he's seen what I can see, but a second later I realise he's just stood back to let his mate do the dirty work. The first punch to my stomach doubles me over and then I take another blow to the back of my neck. I hit the ground, completely helpless. My cheek scrapes on wet gravel as they pile in with their feet. My body jerks with each kick, to my stomach, my back, my neck, my head. I try to brace against it, but I can't protect myself. All I can do is hope they won't stick me with the knife. I close my eyes and curl up as tight as I can until they stop.

I don't know if they think I've had enough or they just get bored, but eventually the kicking stops. I hear them walking away, their footsteps fading and then disappearing. I stay curled up for a while, on the wet ground with the rain falling on the side of my head, starting to soak through my clothes. Blood trickles out of my mouth. I feel like a bit of rubbish someone's dropped. Something left behind. Unwanted. Something to step over.

I'm cold and wet. Very cold, like I was lying in thick snow, not on a damp path.

Cee. Cee, can you hear me, you bastard?

It's not the gang. Only one person calls me Cee. And now I smell him, smell the sharp sour twang of muddy lake.

Can you hear me?

I open my eyes a little way, so there's a narrow slit to see out of, and he's there, half a metre away.

White face, streaked with mud. The face that got zipped into the bag. My eyes open wide. My breathing goes shallow and fast.

I close my eyes again. I'm not seeing this. It isn't real. It's the beating I've taken messing up my head.

'Everywhere. He's everywhere, isn't he?' That's what Mum said.

She sees him too, in her mind's eye. I've got to remember that. I must be concussed, like I was after the lake. Confused. I'll wake up properly soon and he'll have gone.

I open my eyes again. He's lying on the ground like me, his body parallel to mine, but he's naked except for his boxers. There's not a spare ounce on him. I can see his ribs moving under his skin as he lies there gasping and the hedge behind him, dark stems and leaves. Shit! I can see *through* him.

He makes a gurgling noise, a wet rasping as he moves his mouth and water trickles out.

You owe me, little brother, he says.

My head's telling me not to believe this. Not to trust my own senses.

My heart's beating fast and strong.

My poor punched, kicked, bruised and beaten guts twist inside me.

This isn't happening. My brother's dead. My brother is dead.

I stretch my arm across the gap between us. My fingers pass through his shoulder. There's no resistance, nothing there. But that's not quite true, because my hand is aching with cold, like I was holding it in a freezer.

I pull my hand back sharply, revolted by him, horrified.

'What did I do?'

His body convulses. He draws his knees in and jerks his head forwards. Water gushes out of his mouth. Its foul stench fills my nostrils.

I scramble to my feet. He's still lying there, twisting and twitching like a fish out of water, retching and gasping. He's lying at my feet, in the grip of something terrible. He's no threat, surely. But I've never been so terrified.

I can't watch him. I can't stay here.

He splutters again, *You did this. You'll pay, you little runt.*

And I turn and start running.

NINE

I run through wet alleyways and footpaths, under yellow streetlights, through the driving rain, trying to leave him behind. The thing. The Rob that isn't Rob.

But he's with me all the way.

He appears out of nowhere in front of me and suddenly I find myself running towards him, not away. I veer into the road, increasing my pace. But he's everywhere in the shadows. Oh God. Oh God.

Where are you going, Cee?

I realise my feet are still taking me towards Neisha's. I'm desperate to get there, get away from this nightmare, but I can't run any faster. My ankle is still sore from my flying leap off the stairs. My stomach and ribs hurt from the beating. I can't get enough air into my lungs. There's adrenaline surging through me but I can feel my strength sapping away.

I cross the bridge over the river, and turn the corner into River Terrace. It's a wide tree-lined street, Victorian terraces set back from the road, each house with its own pretty garden. And he's here, waiting by the solid stone gatepost at the entrance to Neisha's. I screech to a halt ten metres away.

He says nothing, just stares at me. What does he want? Am I going mad? I've got to walk past him to get to her door, and that fills me with dread.

The house, standing in the middle of the terrace, is dark except for one light somewhere behind the stained glass in the front door. The light's reflected on the polished tiles of the step. The curtains are open. Perhaps everyone's out.

I'm wondering how to get past Rob when he starts coughing. He buckles forward, water pouring from his mouth, and stands there with his head hanging over the pavement. Real or not, I don't want to get any nearer than I have to. I take my chance and vault over the low wall into the front garden.

The ground is wet and slippery under my feet, the rain still hammering down. I stand by the window and look inside. Light from the hallway is shining softly into the lounge, throwing a gentle glow on to a couple of big sofas, a tiled fireplace with vases and ornaments on the mantelpiece above. It's just under a mile away from home, but it's a million miles from a shitty flat like ours ... What the hell was Neisha doing with Rob? Why would someone like her talk to people like us?

At first I think that the room is empty, but then I see

that a discarded coat on one sofa has hands and a head and hair. It's Neisha, curled in a ball, with her knees drawn up to her stomach. Her face is resting on her hands; her palms are together like she's saying a prayer. Her eyes are closed and it feels wrong looking in at her … but I don't want to stop. She's beautiful.

Even in her sleep she looks troubled. Her face is twitching. I lean closer and my foot tips off the edge of the lawn into the flower bed, throwing me off balance. I put my hands out to stop myself and they slap against the window. I curse at my clumsiness.

Neisha gasps and jumps to her feet. She claps one hand to her mouth, trying to stifle a scream, and starts backing away, then turns and runs out of the room. I push on the glass to right myself and step back into the middle of the lawn, my feet sinking into the soft, wet ground. I look at the front of the house, then go up to the door. The porch gives some protection against the rain. I crouch down and peer though the letterbox. She isn't there.

'Neisha!' I shout. 'Neisha, please talk to me.'

Nothing.

'Neisha. I didn't mean to frighten you. Open up, please. I need to talk.'

I bob down and squint through the letterbox again. There's a doorway at the end of the hall. Neisha's hand is clasping the door frame. That's all I can see of her. Just her fingers curled around the edge of the wood.

I turn my head sideways so I can see through the gap with one eye and still shout. Behind me I can hear the faint sound of liquid hitting the pavement. The sound of my dead brother vomiting his guts up. It's not real, I tell myself. It's just the pounding of the rain … but I know if I turn round, he'll be there, with foul stuff pouring out of him.

'Neisha, I know you're there. Come on, please talk to me. You don't have to open the door, if you don't want to.'

Force the door, Cee. Smash it.

His voice is no more than a whisper, but it terrifies me. I can't look round. Oh God, Neisha, please open the door. Let me in. Get me away from the nightmare that's followed me here. Get me away from my own madness.

Rob's groaning quietly now, and each noise twists my guilt tighter inside me. Did I do this to him? Did I really kill him? My guts are so churned up, I feel sick too, like I did in the kitchen. There's pressure building up inside.

When I hear Neisha's voice, it's shaky and quiet.

'Go away, Carl. I'm calling the police.'

She's still hiding. Her disembodied voice echoes in the hallway.

'No, don't! I want to say sorry,' I shout. 'I'm so, so sorry.'

'Sorry's not enough,' she says. 'Sorry's just a word.'

There's a hard edge of bitterness there.

'But I mean it,' I say. 'I know I can't bring him back' — even though, right at this moment he's spewing his guts up behind me — 'but I am really, really sorry.'

'Bring him back?' She sounds confused all of a sudden.

'Yeah, you know …'

'Carl, what exactly are you saying sorry for?'

'For Rob. For killing him.'

Silence.

Then, 'You killed Rob?'

My head's starting to cartwheel. This is what she was mad about, scared about, surely. The stuff in my stomach is pushing its way up.

'Yeah,' I say, 'at least I think so. I can't remember, not everything.'

'Shit.'

I don't get it. If she doesn't think I killed him, why is she so scared? What's going on?

'What did you think I was saying sorry for?'

'For God's sake, Carl!'

'Neisha, I can't remember. Honestly. What happened? Why did you tell the cops we were larking around?'

There's a long pause. Her hand grips the door frame more tightly. I realise I'm holding my breath.

'You tried to kill *me*.'

The cartwheels are sickeningly fast, everything I thought I knew turns upside down, spinning, reeling.

I killed my brother *and* I tried to kill this girl?

'But ... but why would I do something like that?'

'You don't remember *anything*?'

'Just little bits. Fighting with Rob in the lake.'

'You and your evil brother. You were in it together. Now can you see why I don't want you here? I don't want you coming here, Carl. Ever.'

I let the letterbox flip closed and I sink to my knees. No wonder she screamed when she saw me in the ambulance. No wonder she slammed down the phone. Water drips from the edge of the porch roof on to my head, splashing the side of my face. Rob's face flashes out of the darkness and it seems like he's grinning, his mouth a grotesque scar across his pale face.

'For God's sake, go away. Leave me alone!'

I'm shouting at something, someone, that doesn't exist … or does he?

Saliva floods into my mouth and I can't hold on any longer. I tip sideways and vomit into the flower bed. Cold water, again, with the same sour rankness as before. I spit and wipe my mouth on my sleeve, then I pick myself up and start walking. I keep my eyes firmly down.

The rain's still coming, but I don't even feel it. I'm numb.

TEN

There's one word in my head.

Evil.

I don't want to believe Neisha, but why would she lie? She's terrified. I terrify her.

Neisha thinks I'm evil. And I don't know any different. There's only one other person who could tell me if she's right.

The rain trickles down my face and I shiver. I look round for Rob, but for the moment I can't see him.

I stumble on, hardly noticing where I walk, ending up in the town centre, rain bouncing in the gutters. Nearly all the shops are closed. People are hurrying home. I scan the street. He was here before. I didn't know it was him then, but it must have been. Darting in front of me. Ducking into the doorway.

So where is he?

I walk past the shops and turn into the square of old people's bungalows. There's no one about here. Doors are closed. Curtains are shut.

And now I see him. He's pacing backwards and forwards in the middle of the path.

Even though I was looking for him, my stomach lurches. There's something sickeningly edgy about him, like he's full of a demonic power. Backwards and forwards, like a tiger in a zoo. He's muttering to himself, but I can't hear the words.

He turns his face to me.

'Did we do it? Did we try to kill her?' I shout.

Now I hear him.

Kill her. Kill her.

Is he repeating what I've said, or talking to himself? What's going on?

The rain spit-spots on my face. The smudges that are where Rob's eyes should be narrow. Two dark slits. Soundlessly, he walks toward me, face looming up to mine. Close, closer, closer still. I back away but he's faster. I stagger into a doorway, banging my head back on the wood behind. He's coming. I can't stop him.

At the last moment I flinch, and close my eyes, anticipating the crunch as he smashes into me … but feel nothing except an ice-cold draught, cutting through me, penetrating my bones.

'Jesus!'

I open my eyes, and he's gone.

I look all the way down the road. No one. An empty

street, tarmac glistening in the streetlight.

'Rob!' I shout out. 'I need to know!'

But he's gone. Suddenly the door I'm leaning on gives way and there's a guy standing there, clasping a poker like a sword. He's an old fella, wearing a checked shirt tucked into impressively high-waisted trousers, held up with leather braces. There are slippers on his feet.

'Clear off,' he says. 'Get off out of here.' Then he stops. 'Oh, it's you, Carl.'

He lowers the poker. He knows me. I'm racking my brains trying to think how. What's the connection? The paint on the door isn't wet – the porch has protected it – but it's shiny in the streetlight. Why am I remembering the strong, oily smell of gloss paint?

'How's your mum coping? Worst thing a mother can go through, losing a kid.'

The air coming out from the open door is warm and stuffy. I shiver.

'What's happened to your face, son?'

'Some lads jumped me,' I say. I hear him sigh.

'Fighting?' he says. 'Don't you think your poor mother's got enough to deal with right now?'

I look at him, then, and he sighs again.

'Come on in, son. You need some TCP on that cut.' He nods towards my face. I put my hand up and suck my breath in as my fingers touch a graze on my cheek that I didn't even know was there.

'Nah, I'll do it at home. You're all right.'

'Come on, I owe you for that work you did in the summer. You did a good job of my front door.'

'I did?'

'Huh,' he chuckles, 'I thought I was the one with the dicky memory. I'm Harry, remember? The school sent you. You and your mates. Community action or something – I don't know what they call it – but you were a big help to me. I can't do the things I used to, you know.'

It's not quite there, but the memory's not far away either. I stand in the doorway while he turns away, heading inside.

In the hall facing the door are two rows of coat hooks, a dog lead and a collar hanging on the lower row. My hands reach forward, picking up the collar off the hook, turning it round in my hands, and my mind spins back to a dark night, a bungalow that we thought was empty.

We don't even have to break in – the back door isn't locked. Rob's in front of me. I can hear barking.

'Winston?' A woman's voice.

'Rob, get out! Get out now!'

It was here. This was the bungalow. The dog that barked – this was his collar.

'Close the door behind you,' Harry says, reappearing from the kitchen at the back. He stops as he sees me with the collar in my hands. 'Put that back, please,' he says and there's something in his voice that makes me do what he says, quick smart.

'I … I'm sorry.'

He keeps looking at me, and I'm starting to sweat. I can feel a confession trying to elbow its way out of me.

'I … I …'

'All right, son,' he says. 'Don't touch it again, that's all.

It's not yours. Have you still got that book I gave you?'

'Book?'

'*Of Mice and Men*, wasn't it? That's a good one. I loved that book when I was your age.'

I breathe out. So it was him. In a flash of memory I remember being here before, seeing it on his shelf, picking it up because we were doing it at school. I told him someone had nicked mine and he said, 'You can have that one. I don't need it any more.'

I couldn't believe someone would just give me something like that.

'Yeah,' I say, 'I've still got it. I love it too.'

He smiles and I wish I could smile back, but this is cutting me in two, because of that other time, the time Rob and me came back here.

'Now, come into the light, in the kitchen,' he says. 'I'll be able to see that scrape properly.'

Not the kitchen. Not where …

'Come on,' he says, 'don't just stand there.'

He shuffles down the hallway. I could cut and run now, but I don't. He's got his back to me, rummaging in a cupboard. I stand just outside the doorway scanning the floor. What did I expect? Two painted outlines highlighting where the bodies lay, a woman and a dog? The rotting remains still in a heap? There's nothing here. No marks, no dents, no smears, no spatters. It's lino, pretending to be black and white tiles.

'Come in,' he says, 'I won't bite.'

His voice is drowned out by the voice of his wife in my head. '*You bastard. You thieving, cowardly bastard.*'

'I should go,' I say.

'Yes, all right. After I've fixed you up a bit. Come here.' He beckons me towards him. 'Get under this light.'

I move forward until I'm standing on the exact spot where the dog was lying. It feels like the floor is moving underneath my feet, like there's a paw or an ear or something trapped under there. I shift a little bit to the side.

'Here, stop moving about. Stand still.'

He's close now, and the smell of his minty breath mixes with the sharp tang of the disinfectant that's soaking the ball of cotton wool in his hands. He brings it up towards me. Close to, I can see all the wear and tear in his skin, the way the whites of his eyes aren't white, but yellow. I close my eyes and flinch as the TCP makes contact with my raw cut.

''S'all right,' he says. 'Nearly done. There, you can open your eyes now. I'm finished. Do you want a cup of tea?'

I should go. I shouldn't be here. Despite this, I nod.

'Go and sit down in the lounge, son.'

I walk through. It's tiny, neat and tidy … and familiar. A patterned carpet. Woodchip on the walls. Bookshelves either side of the fire. And photographs. I walk over to the mantelpiece and look along the row of pictures. Some are of people on their own, others are group shots. I pick up one with just two people in it; the old man and a woman, his wife. There's a caption along the bottom – *Harry & Iris, 22nd July 2012.*

They are looking straight at the camera, side by side. Heads leaning towards each other, Harry's hand just showing where he's got his arm round her shoulder, holding her close. They're both togged up – him in a tweed jacket, white shirt and tie, her in a glossy blouse with a bow loosely tied at the neck. Nestling in the shiny material is a necklace – a silver locket on a chain.

I'm walking across the park with Neisha. She's nervously touching the silver locket that's swinging on a chain around her neck.

'Golden wedding, that was.' Harry's voice makes me jump and jerk my head round to look over my shoulder. I'm ready to be told off again for touching, but he doesn't seem to mind this time. He's standing in the doorway holding a tea tray.

'Fifty years,' he says. 'Fifty years ... thought we might make it to diamond, but ... That's the last photo we had taken together.'

'What happened?'

'Don't you remember that either, son?'

'I'm sorry, I've been in hospital. They said I got concussion in the lake.'

'Ah, nasty. You'll get better, though, son.'

'Yeah, it's getting better already. I've just got some ... gaps. I'm sorry about your wife ... Iris?'

'I haven't seen you since it happened. You haven't been round ...'

'So ...?'

He puts the tray down on a table and starts pouring hot steaming tea into two mugs. I don't think he's heard me or understood what I'm asking, but when he's handed me my tea and settled into an armchair with his, he starts talking.

'I'd gone out to fetch some indigestion tablets. She ...

Iris ... had been feeling a bit off. I wasn't gone long, twenty minutes or so. The chemist's wasn't open so I called round at the neighbour's.

'I found them in the kitchen. Iris and the dog, both ... both ... you know. Doctor said it was a heart attack. That's why she was feeling dicky earlier. Said she must've found poor old Winston and that was it. It was too much for her – probably would have happened anyway. Natural causes. But there's something bothering me, something not right.'

Up to now he's been looking at the photo on the mantelpiece, but now he turns and leans towards me in his chair.

'Her necklace was gone. She always wore it. A silver locket on a chain. She's wearing it in that photo. It was one I gave her on our first anniversary – twenty-second of July 1962 – she put it on and never took it off. Now I can't find it.'

His eyes are red-rimmed.

'Things get lost,' I say, trying not to squirm in my seat.

He shakes his head.

'No, not this.' He dabs at his face with a big white hankie. 'Someone was in here.'

His words hang in the air between us.

'I'd better go home.' I splutter, through a mouthful of tea. 'Mum'll be wondering where I am.'

He puts his hankie away.

'Good lad,' he says, 'you look after your mum. Terrible thing, to lose someone so young.'

He follows me down the hall and lets me out. It's dry

outside now; dry and dark and quiet. I pause on his doorstep, scanning around for signs of Rob, half expecting him to be waiting there. He isn't.

'Thanks for the tea,' I say.

I turn and walk down the path. When I look back, he's still standing there, watching me. He raises his hand briefly and shuts the door.

I pull my hood up and head for home. I keep my eyes peeled all the way, but Rob's nowhere to be seen.

ELEVEN

Mum's not on the sofa. She's on the kitchen floor, on her hands and knees. From where I'm standing I can see her backside resting on her heels, wiggling from side to side.

'Mum? What the—?'

She doesn't seem to hear me. She's scrubbing the lino, going at it so manically her whole body's moving.

'Mum?' I try again.

This time she twists round. Her hair's flopping into her eyes. She huffs out of her open mouth, making the hair waft out for a second before it flops back again.

'In a minute, Carl, I've just got to get this done.'

She's wiping the same patch of floor, over and over again. She starts to cry, then sits up on her heels and scrapes some hair out of the way with the back of her hand.

'Where've you been all evening, Carl?' she says.

'What difference does it make?'

'What difference? What difference?! I'm your bloody mum, in case you hadn't noticed. I should know where you are. If I'd known where you were, perhaps … perhaps …' She can't bring herself to say it. 'Rob was a good swimmer. What happened, Carl?'

In the water, I lock my arms around his neck, holding my elbows in a vice-like grip, making a double layer of skin and bone. I bring them back towards me, pulling on his neck, compressing.

'I can't remember, Mum. I told you. I can't hardly remember anything about it.'

'But why were you there?'

'If I knew, I'd tell you, right?' I'm nearly shouting, fuelled by the confusion, the disbelief, the guilt that's been building up all day.

She goes back to scrubbing the floor, tears running down her face.

'Cleaning the floor won't bring him back.' The words are out before I can stop them.

She's leaning on one hand, head down, face hidden. She looks pathetic, broken. And I suddenly remember what Harry said, 'Worst thing a mother can go through, losing a kid.' And I feel ashamed.

I find another cloth under the sink and kneel down next to her.

'Here, let me help you.'

I let her carry on polishing her clean patch, and steadily work my way round her. As I dip the cloth into the bucket, a shiver runs down my spine.

We nearly did it, Cee.

A voice, his voice, close to my ear.

I look round. It's just Mum and me, on the kitchen floor.

I take a few deep breaths and carry on working. Where my fingers grip the cloth, water oozes out. The voice is still there — cold, quiet, chilling.

Nearly's not enough.

Jesus. Something clicks in the back of my brain. Something to do with the moisture on my fingers ... and Rob — here one minute and gone the next.

I spring up.

'I reckon that's done it, Mum. Do you want a drink?' I say.

She sits up on her heels and looks around her.

'Coffee,' she says. 'Black coffee would be nice.'

I empty the bucket into the sink. The filthy water splashes my arms and the twang of decay catches at the back of my mouth, making me gag.

Mum sits at the table, pushes the heap of leaflets to one side. I make coffee for her and sit down.

'Since when have you drunk coffee?'

'Cheeky sod,' she says, but she's almost smiling. 'That's it now. This is what I'm going to drink. I'm on the wagon.'

I force myself to meet her eyes. A thread of red runs through the white of her right eye, the skin underneath is puffy and saggy.

'I mean it. This is it, Carl. I got things wrong, terribly wrong. I've been a bad person.' Her eyes are brimming with tears again.

'Mum, don't ...'

We sit in silence.

'I might have a bath,' she says after a while. 'You should have one too – you're filthy. I'll leave the water in for you.'

'Okay,' I say, but there's no way I'm getting in a bath. My head's full of horror, seeing a body lying under the surface of the bathwater; pale, still, hair floating out, away from his head. Dead, but not dead.

Mum drains her mug, tipping her head right back to get all the dregs, and gets up to go to the bathroom. I hear her make her way upstairs. The sound of water running brings back the fear, like cockroaches running all over my body.

Upstairs, I hide in my sleeping bag, curling up with my back turned to the dark stain on the ceiling. If I'm asleep, or Mum thinks I am when she gets out of the bath, perhaps she'll leave me be.

But I can't sleep. Everything that's happened today is tumbling around my head. I can't make sense of it.

Instinctively, I reach for my book, the comfort of reading. And I understand now why it means so much to me. It's not just the story, it's the book itself. The fact that Harry gave it to me. And it wasn't even my birthday.

'A water snake slipped along on the pool, its head held up like a little periscope. The reeds jerked slightly in the current.'

I close the book again, and let it flop on to the floor.

There are questions snaking through my head, things too awful to think about. Things that I can't stop thinking about.

How could I betray Harry and burgle his house? How

did I end up fighting my brother in a lake? How did he end up dead? Did I really want Neisha – lovely, beautiful Neisha – dead too?

Am I a killer?

TWELVE

I wake up in yesterday's clothes, yesterday's dirt. Now I lie on my back looking at the dark patch on the ceiling; it's grown again. I can hear voices downstairs, female voices. I haul myself out of bed and pad into the kitchen.

I do a double take. Neisha's standing in the kitchen with her back to me, talking to Mum. She's got a thigh-length black coat on, fitted so it goes in at the waist. There are tiny specks of rain sitting on the surface of the fabric, the same with her hair.

Why's she here?

Oh God, I look like a tramp. Our flat looks like a dosshouse.

I'm about to sneak away, but Mum's seen me, and her eye movement alerts Neisha. She turns round and a tight little smile blinks on and off.

'All right,' I say, half in, half out of the doorway.

'Hey,' she says. The whites of her eyes flash as she quickly looks at me and looks away, turning straight back to Mum. She's faking it, trying to pretend she wants to be here, but even that half a second of eye contact is enough to melt me, turn me to jelly.

'I wanted to say ... to say how sorry I am. About Rob,' she says.

What? I think back to last night in the rain outside her house.

'Thanks, love,' Mum says. She looks better for her bath. Her hair's clean, tied back into a neat ponytail, but her face is still crumpled, her eyes are still puffy. 'I appreciate that. I appreciate you coming. How are you doing? It must be difficult for you.'

'Oh, I'm ... you know.'

Terrified? Terrified of your sons! What's she doing here?

'I was lucky, I suppose, I had him for seventeen years. You'd only just got together. You had your whole lives ahead of you. It's so cruel.'

There's a little pause where I guess Neisha's trying to pick the right words, and I think, *please don't say anything bad, not to Mum*. Then she says tightly, 'We had a few months. I'll always remember them. Always remember him.'

She glances back nervously to me, as Mum steps forward and puts her arms round her. She's wrapping Neisha up in her arms and I wonder how Neisha can do it, let this woman hold her, this woman whose sons tried to kill her. It's weird seeing Mum like this, too. I can't remember ever having a hug from her.

Behind them the tap is dripping into the kitchen sink, a steady feed of drops that's on the edge of being a stream.

When Mum steps back, they've both got tears in their eyes. 'Do you want a drink? Some Coke or a cup of tea?' Mum says.

Neisha checks back at me. I shrug. I don't know why she's here, how long she's planning to stay.

'Um ...'

'It's okay,' Mum says. 'I'll make myself scarce.'

Neisha smiles again, a quick, brittle smile that betrays her nerves.

'Okay,' she says, 'I'll just have some water.'

Mum fetches a glass and fills it at the tap. She turns the tap as far as it will go, but it still keeps dripping.

'I'll leave you to it,' she says. 'I'll be upstairs.' On her way past me, she hisses, 'The state of you. You're going in that bath today.'

Neisha and I stand awkwardly either side of the kitchen table.

'Sit down,' I say, trying to be polite, but it comes out like an order. I wince at my own clumsiness and dart round to pull out one of the chairs for her. Instinctively, she takes a step backwards. 'Please,' I say, retreating back to my own side, and reluctantly she lowers herself down, perching nervously on the edge of the chair.

I sit down opposite her. The pile of leaflets is still there. I wish it wasn't, but if I pick them up now, it'll just draw attention to them. Too late, anyway, Neisha's seen them, her eyes are tracking across the titles.

I try to think of something to say, anything, to distract her.

'You were nice, just then, to my mum.'

'Why wouldn't I be? It's not her fault, is it? All of this ...'

Not her fault. My fault. Has she just come round to have another go?

'Neisha——' I say.

'What?' Her eyes flick up and down nervously.

'I'm sorry. For everything. I don't remember much, but the stuff I do remember is ...' I trail off, then I say the thing I'm really thinking. 'Why are you here? You hate me, don't you? I tried to ... me and Rob tried to ...'

Then she does something that makes me gasp. She reaches across and puts her hand on my wrist. Her touch is light and her skin is warm, shockingly warm. I feel myself blushing, blotches forming on my face and neck. I can't look at her. If I look at her I might actually explode.

'The thing is,' she says, 'I've come round to thank you.'

And now I do look at her. As our eyes meet, I get a flash of another time. When I was looking at her, and she saw me looking.

He slides his hands down her sides, around to the front. I stand and watch him stroke her, squeeze her, turn her on. She sees me over his shoulder. For a second I wonder if there's a question there, an appeal for help, but then her eyes close and her mouth opens.

I stand. And watch. And I can't believe it.

She's back with him. After everything that's happened.

He breaks away from her and starts peeling off his clothes. Down to his underpants, he runs into the water until it's up to his knees.

'Come on,' he shouts. *She shakes her head, but then arches her back as she peels off her top, and I can't look any more. Disgusted, humiliated, I turn away.*

'Carl, are you listening? I wanted to thank you.'

'Thank me?'

'I've been thinking about what you said. How you said you killed him. Rob.'

She lowers her voice even further. Her fingers tighten a little, curving over the back of my hand.

'I think I did. I'm not sure. I remember fighting him.' I lower my voice too. 'My arms were pulling on his neck.'

'I didn't know what had happened,' she says. 'All I can remember is that we'd swum further than I wanted to, way out of my depth. I wanted to go back, but he stopped me and then ...' she starts to stumble on the words, ' ... then he ripped the necklace off me, he put his hands round my throat. He was strangling me, and you were swimming towards us, shouting. And he let go. The thing is ... you must be telling the truth. Why would he let go unless someone forced him to? Unless you forced him to? You probably saved my life, Carl.'

Can that be true? Am I the one who saved her?

'Did you see what happened next?'

'No. As soon as he let go, I started swimming away. I didn't even know where, just away. And it was raining so much I couldn't see anyway. I could hear you, though, the two of you ... swearing at each other, splashing, getting fainter the further I swam ... I made it to the shore, and a few minutes later, so did you.'

'But you said before that I tried to kill you. Me and my evil brother.'

'I was confused. It was all so quick. I was in shock. I thought you were in on it, that you knew what he was going to do. You see, he had some photos of me, on his phone.' She's looking down at our hands on the table, now, can't meet my eye. 'He said he'd show my dad if I didn't meet him. And you said – don't you remember? – you said that he'd really do it, that I had to go to the lake and see him, but you'd protect me. You'd meet me from school and we'd walk there together. And then you'd stay in the bushes nearby while I talked to him.'

Walking across the grass together. She touches the silver locket at her neck.

'But at the lake, you kissed him,' I say. 'I saw you. You both took your clothes off, you went in the water … you were back together with him, Neisha.'

'Because he said that if I didn't do exactly what he told me to, he'd put the photos on the Internet, he'd print them and send them to my dad … he'd turn up at home if he needed to. I was scared, Carl. I had no choice. So I did it. I took my clothes off … and when I looked round for you, you were walking away. I thought you'd betrayed me.'

'But then I saw you in the water, struggling, and I came to help. To get him off you.'

'Yes. I really think you did. You were looking out for me after all, Carl. Like you always did. You never betrayed me, and thank God you were there, or else … I would've …'

I saved her? I'm her hero. Rob was trying to kill her. Him, not me.

She takes a sip from her glass. A drop spills on the table. It sits on the formica surface, a tiny dome of water. It's nothing, just a drop. I put my fingertip on it and try to smear it away and suddenly my head is full of him.

Don't listen to the bitch.

His voice in my ears. The harsh twang of lake water in my nostrils. A chill running down my spine.

I wipe my finger on the leg of my jeans and it all stops. I'm right about the water. I must be.

Neisha brings the glass up to her lips again and my stomach turns inside out as the water passes from the glass into her mouth. Water. In the tap, in the lake, on her lips, in her mouth. Her hardly-there Adam's apple bobs up and down as she swallows. And now I notice a vivid red line around the side of her neck, where the chain must have bitten deep into her skin.

She mustn't drink the water. I reach forward and take the glass from her hand. She's too surprised to resist.

'What are you doing?'

'Don't drink it,' I say.

'What?'

'It's dirty. I just noticed – the glass is dirty.' I quickly take it away and put it in the sink.

She scrapes her chair back, but doesn't stand up. 'I'd better go anyway.'

She's biting her bottom lip and I know she's got something else to say. I wait, letting the silence hang between us.

'Carl, I know this is terrible for you. If you did kill him, you did an awful thing. But you did it to stop something else bad happening. And I'm really, really grateful.' She's looking down, at her hands clasped in her lap. As she speaks, her fingers squeeze hard. She's squashing her hands out of shape. 'The thing is, you're a good person and I should have listened to you. Should have kept away from him from the start. All of this, it's not all on your shoulders. I'm guilty too.'

'What do you mean?' I say. 'You're not guilty of anything. He tried to kill you.'

'I made him do it.'

'What?'

'I pushed him too far.'

She checks up at me briefly and looks back down again.

'I don't understand.' I say. I sit down at the table.

'You really don't remember, do you?' She sighs.

'I feel like I'm going mad not knowing what's going on, what happened.' My voice is louder than I intended and she looks up, startled. She's chewing at her lip again. When she speaks, it's so quiet I can hardly hear her.

'I threatened him. I threatened to tell his secrets. Secrets that could get him in a lot of trouble.'

THIRTEEN

'I'd tried to break away from him so many times, but I always went back. He'd say sorry, talk me round. I believed him each time. Believed he was sorry. Sometimes, when I was upset, I'd talk to you. You were always there for me. You'd listen. But Rob thought it was more than that. He was jealous, really jealous. I tried to tell him it was all in his head, but he went mad. Then I knew I had to keep him away from me, for good this time, so I told him that if he came near me again I'd tell all the things I knew about him. Things that would get him in trouble. Sent to prison.'

'What things?' I say. Her hand goes up to her neck.

'He gave me that locket and he told me where it came from. Do you remember that, Carl?'

I nod.

'The old woman,' I say. 'The one that died.'

'Me, you and Rob, we were the only ones who knew about it,' Neisha says. 'I told him that I'd tell the police about the necklace if he didn't leave me alone.'

'But why do something like that? Threaten him? Couldn't you just break things off and keep out of his way?'

She gives a little snort through her nose.

'Sounds easy when you put it like that. But you can't go anywhere, do anything, in this town without bumping into people. You can't avoid people unless you just shut yourself away. I did that, too, though, believe me.'

'So he wanted to keep you quiet, that's why he—'

She nods. 'Yes, but it was the jealousy, too. He thought that you were … we were … you know … behind his back.'

'But we weren't … were we? And he didn't kill the old lady, Neisha. That's not how it was. Rob killed the dog, and the old woman was screaming and crying about it. Then she kind of … collapsed. It was horrible, and I hated him for making me go with him to burgle Harry's, just 'cos I knew the layout, where all the valuables were. But he didn't kill her.'

She looks at me sharply.

'That's not what Rob said. He said he'd done her. Used those words. *Done her.* And no, you and I weren't at it. You're too nice for an idiot like me. We were just friends.'

I run my hands through my hair, starting to doubt the memories that have come back to me. 'But what I don't get is, if that's what he told you — that he killed her — why did you stay with him? Why did you keep going back to him? Was it just the photos?'

She sighs and, leaning her elbows on the table, holds her head in her hands, mirroring me.

'No, that was towards the end. I don't know. I don't know.'

But she does know, she's just not saying.

'You thought he was a murderer, and you went back ...'

There are tears seeping into her eyelashes. I want to stop this, make it better, hold her. But I need to know.

'You went back, Neisha. Why?'

She looks up. Her lips are pressed into a thin line.

'I was scared. He told me he'd kill me if I left him. And I knew he could kill. I knew he was violent. You saw what he did to me.'

The red line around her neck.

'In the lake?'

'And before. That's why you and I became close.'

'It was my fault, Carl.'

The mark on her face is showing through her make-up. A dark shadow that won't stay hidden.

'No. It can never be your fault. You didn't make him do that. It's wrong.'

'I upset him. I was nagging. He told me to stop.'

'He was born upset, Neisha. Trust me, I know.'

Another gap starts to fill in my brain.

Neisha holds her forehead with her hand, squeezing at the temples. 'It wasn't just that old woman. He hit me. Remember? He hurt me.'

There's a noise from the hallway. A soft thud. Neisha

and I look questioningly at each other and then I jump up and go to look. Mum's there, bending down to pick up a pile of magazines.

'You all right?' I say.

She looks up at me and her face is flustered, caught in the act. How long has she been there? How much did she hear?

I was just ... just going to put these in the recycling,' she says.

Neisha's next to me in the doorway, pushing past.

'I'd better go,' she says.

'No,' I say, 'no, not now. Please. Please stay.'

I reach out and put my hand on her arm, and she flinches.

A set of dull grey bruises on the soft part of her arm, between her wrist and elbow. She thinks I haven't seen, but I have.

'He shouldn't do that to you.'

She looks away. I reach out and take her hand in mine. It's soft and warm.

'I would never, ever hurt you, Neisha.'

I move my hand away, but I follow her to the door. Mum stands and watches us, magazines in hand. It's raining, a soft, soundless drizzle, drifting about in the air. It's not much, but it's enough to set butterflies going in my stomach. Neisha pauses on the front step. She turns her collar up around her neck. I stand next to her and pull the door to behind me.

'She heard,' she says.

'Yeah, I think so. I'll talk to her.'

'God, what a mess.'

'It'll be all right,' I say, but my words sound empty and foolish.

The concrete walls and walkway look greyer than ever in the rain. A drip from the ledge hits my hand, and someone, something, flits across the far end of the walkway, near the top of the stairs. I pull my arms in close to my body, flatten myself against the door.

'What are you doing?' Neisha says. 'Are you hiding?'

'No. No, 'course not.'

I want to tell her, I really do. But not yet.

She looks over her shoulder.

'Is someone there?'

'No, there's no one.'

She checks behind her again. I guess if you're not used to it, it would feel threatening round here.

'Will you walk me to the end?' she says. She's looking at me, waiting.

'Sure,' I say and I step out from under the canopy. The rain is so light it's hardly there at all. There are no sudden movements, no voices in my ear, and my fear starts subsiding. Neisha links her arm through mine and, even through her coat, I'm aware of her warmth.

'I'll walk you home, shall I?' I say.

She looks across at me.

'You'd better stay and talk to your mum,' she says.

'But we need to talk, you and me,' I say.

'I know,' she says, 'and we will, but we need to know how much she heard, what she's going to do. She could go to the police, couldn't she? You could be in trouble.'

I shrug.

'I dunno. I don't think it's likely. If she heard what he did to you, I reckon she'll keep quiet. It happened to her, see. Not Rob, our dad. He hurt her. It's how she lost the end of her finger. I was defending you in the lake, trying to protect you, so I don't think she'll tell.' We're nearly at the end of the walkway. The rain is so soft, I hardly notice it, but my face and neck and hands are moist. 'Neisha, why did you tell them what you did? That we were just larking about? Why didn't you tell them the truth?'

'I was scared of you. You persuaded me to meet him. I thought you were in it together. I thought you'd come after me if I said anything.'

I feel like someone's scooped out my insides. The thought of her being scared of me – I can't stand it.

'And I'd have had to tell everything,' she says, 'everything I just told you. I just couldn't do it.'

'I don't understand. You didn't do anything wrong. He hurt you. You were trying to protect yourself.'

'It sounds so simple when you say it like that. It's not simple when you're in the middle of it. It feels like … like it's your fault. And you feel … ashamed.'

She looks away. I stop walking and put my hand on her other arm, gently turning her to face me. She still won't look me in the eye.

'It wasn't your fault. None of this was your fault. My God, Neisha …'

I want to put my arms round her. I want to draw her close.

There's something pale in the stairwell. It's blurry, indistinct, just a suggestion of a shape.

I freeze.

It's coming out of the gloom, heading straight for us.

Neisha turns her head to face me. 'What is it?' she says.

The shape is human. It's only half there, but I know who it is. And he's angry. Really angry.

'Run!' I shout. 'Quick, back to the flat!'

I start to drag Neisha back along the walkway. I've got to get her inside.

She's screaming, 'What's going on? What is it?'

We blast in through the front door, staggering into the hall. Mum's not there any more. I grab a towel from the kitchen and rub my hair, my face.

'It's the rain. The rain—'

I hold the towel out to Neisha. She's hovering by the open door, wide-eyed. Rob isn't there. He hasn't followed us in. We're safe.

'No, it's all right,' she says. 'I hardly got wet. What's wrong? You're frightening me.'

What's wrong? What is wrong? She doesn't know; she can't see what I see. I think I know what's going on now, but I need to be sure before I tell – if …

'It's nothing,' I say. 'I'm just jumpy about rain, ever since … you know.'

'Stay in, then. Stay here. I'll be all right.'

'Well, at least take an umbrella. Don't get wet, Neisha.' I can't believe I'm letting her go out alone.

She screws up her eyes a little, like she's going to ask me something else, then she decides against it. 'Calm down, I've got one,' she says, patting her shoulder bag. 'Will you ring me later?'

'Yeah. I will.' I need to know she gets home safe.

'You've got … you've got his phone? It confused me when you rang the first time, it—'

'Yeah, I can't find mine. Maybe it's at the bottom of the lake.'

She's colouring up and then I do too. I can feel the blood surging into my face as I think of the photos. The photos of her.

She looks like she wants to say something, but then she bites her lip, mutters, 'Later, then.' And she slips out of the flat. I hear her walking away, her boots slapping on the wet concrete. I close the door and lean against it for a minute or two, trying to catch my breath, trying to get the kaleidoscope of voices and pictures in my head to settle into some sort of pattern. Something that makes sense.

What Neisha's told me has stunned me. I should be with her – there's so much I want to ask. But she's right, I need to talk to Mum.

'Mum? Where are you?'

'I'm in here.' Her voice is dull, a monotone. She's in the lounge, sitting on the sofa.

The magazines are on the coffee table. She's got something else in her hands now – the old school photo, me and Rob in matching shirts and ties and slicked-down hair. She's muttering under her breath – I can only just catch what she says.

'So young. So young …'

Her son, dead at seventeen. And I killed him.

'I know. I'm sorry.'

She doesn't seem to have heard me.

'... You think it just goes over their heads, but it doesn't. They take it in, even when they're tots. I should've got out earlier. Left the bastard. I never thought ... never thought ...'

She puts the photo down and now she's clasping her hands together, rubbing the end of her short finger with her thumb.

'Mum ...?'

She looks up, sees me framed in the doorway.

'Rob?' she says. 'Oh Rob, what have you done?' She struggles to her feet and steps towards me, frowning, shielding her eyes.

'No, Mum, it's me. Carl.'

I move towards her and we meet in the middle of the room.

'Carl,' she says, like she's trying to remember. 'Carl.' Then her face clears.

'Carl,' she says. She takes both my hands in hers, and now it feels like she's back with me. 'Has the girl gone?' She looks past me, into the hall.

'Yes, she's gone home. How much did you hear?' I ask.

She looks at me, brimming over with confusion.

'Enough,' she says.

'Are you going to turn me in? Are you going to tell anyone? The police?'

'What for?' she says.

'You know what for. I ... killed him.'

'It was an accident,' she says, stubbornly.

'No, Mum. It was a lot of things, but it wasn't an accident. I wouldn't blame you if you did turn me in.'

'We don't do that, Carl. Not in this family. We don't blab. We don't grass.' She looks at me bleakly. 'Besides, what good would it do? I've lost one son, I don't want to lose another.'

'I'm sorry,' I say again.

Her hands tighten on mine, and I feel the end of her little finger on my skin. It's smoother than the other fingers. Something jolts inside me. The pain she's gone through, held inside all these years.

'You did what you had to do,' she says. 'You stood up to him.'

'But I didn't want … I never wanted …'

'I know. But maybe this is the end. A full stop to all the violence. Let's hope so.'

A full stop. But where did it start in the first place? I bring our hands up between us, turn her hand over, so it's palm upwards.

'Rob told me what happened to your finger, Mum.'

She glances at me, a quick bright-eyed flash, and then she looks away. Like Neisha looked away.

'You were just a babe in arms. But Rob … Rob saw it and I wish to God he hadn't. It was an accident. The sort of accident that happened every time your dad had a skinful at the pub.'

The muscles at the corner of her mouth are twitching.

'It's all right, Mum.'

She shakes her head.

'It doesn't matter now. It was a long time ago.'

Her hand is shaking in mine. I bring both her hands behind my back, put them at my waist and I wrap my arms round her. We hold on tightly to each other, rocking gently from side to side, and after a few seconds her body starts shaking as she cries into my shoulder.

Maybe this *is* the end, an end to the violence. It's what she wants to believe, but Rob was here, today, outside in the mist, and he was angry. It's not over yet. I've got a feeling that it's not nearly over.

FOURTEEN

I'm standing in the bathroom, facing the bath with the shower fixed at one end.

Rob.

He's there when I'm wet.

And not when I'm dry.

That's it. I worked it out.

The tap. The rain. The water slopping on to the floor from the bucket.

The drop of water on the table. My finger touching it. Rob's voice.

It isn't just the water being there, it's me being in contact with it.

It doesn't seem to affect Mum or Neisha. Just me.

If I'm right, he'll come to me. Not when I run the water, but when I step in. When my skin is wet.

My guts are churning. What am I doing? He hates me. He's angry, really angry. The last couple of times he's even launched himself at me. My shoulders spasm at the thought.

But he can't hurt me, can he? He's dead. I can just turn him off. Twist the tap, towel myself dry and he'll be gone.

I take a deep breath, drop my clothes in a pile on the floor and step into the bath. Mouldy grout criss-crosses between the tiles. I pick the shower head up from the cradle where it sits. Keeping my back to the wall, I turn on the tap, directing the water straight at the plughole.

My feet are wet. I keep scanning around, but nothing's happening. The water's lukewarm. I twist the dial, so it goes hotter, and move the spray up to my knees.

Where is he?

I hold the shower over my head and close my eyes as it waterfalls off my forehead and down the front of me. I'm in a haze of water, noisy and steamy and soothing. Perhaps I've got it all wrong. Perhaps my mind *has* been playing tricks. Something inside me is desperate for him not to appear, then at least I can get clean, really clean. I grope for the bottle of shampoo and lather up my hair. It's kids' shampoo – for some reason Mum still buys this stuff – and it smells of bananas and melons, like a massacre in a greengrocer's. I tip my head back and let the water rinse the bubbles away, enjoying the feeling as they slide down my skin.

And suddenly the water goes icy cold. The shock is electric. I cry out and try to open my eyes, but the remains of the soap stings them shut again. I frantically splash water against my lids, but it's cold and foul and the stench of it makes me gag.

I open my eyes again through the water, and he's there. Everything's blurry and distorted, seen through a brown haze, but I know it's him.

He's close.

The water isn't bouncing off his body and running down like it is on me. It's running through him. I can even see the black and white grid of tiles behind.

He's looking at me.

He doesn't say a word. There are holes where his eyes should be, dark gaps in his face, and they're so full of anger that I want to look away. I need to look away. But I can't. My guilt paralyses me.

And now it feels like I'm trapped here with him, in this tiny space. We're in a cave of water and the walls are somehow solid. I'm doused in rankness. And we're both silent. Looking.

I'm powerless.

I need to remember something, but I don't know what.

The water pounds down, drilling a hole in my skull, and the cold isn't just on the surface now, on my skin – it's seeping through me, getting into my muscles and bones. It's an ache, a pain; it's infecting me.

I know that the thing I can't remember was important, but it's gone.

My knees buckle and I hit the hard bottom of the bath. The shower twists in my hands and sprays upwards, ricocheting off the ceiling. Water pummels my shoulders and the top of my back. I'm slumped in a vile brown soup at Rob's feet.

All my energy seems to have disappeared in the arctic cold of the water. All I can do is look at my brother. His blue-white feet, the deep red weal round one ankle. Scratches on his face, and scrapes on his knuckles, mud under his nails. I can see it all, every detail.

He's there and not there. Solid and mud-streaked and see-through.

The water is flowing into him and through him and out of him, flooding out from his nose and mouth, oozing from the pores of his skin.

The water on my shoulders is digging in now. Dropping like nails on the same sore patch of skin. I wish I'd never started this.

You owe me, little brother.

He's looking down at me. His mouth doesn't move, but it's his voice. Am I reading his thoughts? Is he reading mine?

'I don't know what you mean. What do you want?' I say. I tip my face up towards his and water batters it, making me flinch and cough.

Now he coughs too, spasms that make his whole body twitch and dance. He crouches next to me, leans to the side and is sick, muddy water gushing out of him, filling the air with its stink. It swirls round my feet and backside.

'What do you want me to do?'

Bring the whore to the lake.

'No!' I don't want to hear any more.

Cee, he says. *Cee, you owe me.*

If I could just remember how to get rid of him. The cold has numbed my brain. The relentlessness of the water drowns out the thoughts that are trying to form.

There's a change in the water around my feet. It seems alive. Rivulets begin to flow up my legs, snaking their way round my ankles and calves. What's happening?

He's closer than ever, looming over me, around me. I turn my head and he's there. I twist away and he's there again. Wherever I look his eyeless sockets are boring into me with their cold, dark power. And the water is flowing into my mouth now, up my nostrils. It's forcing its way into my throat. I'm coughing, choking. How do I make this go away? How can I turn him off?

Turn him off.

That's what I told myself I could do. That's what I needed to remember. I'm in control – all I have to do is turn the tap. I reach behind me. I can't find the tap at first. My fingers grasp at thin air. Where is it? I turn round and my movement must have tilted the shower head because now the water is all falling on my hand. Cold, hard, drops battering against the skin. It's so cold that my joints stiffen. I can't feel the ends of my fingers.

Don't you fucking dare.

I'm still holding the shower in my other hand. I try to angle it away, turn it over so it's facing down, but it slips out of my grip and now it's alive. The metal hose writhes in the bottom of the bath, twisting and turning under the pressure of the water, and at the end of it, the shower head spews out its icy guts and no matter which way out it starts, all the water ends up attacking my hand. It thunders down from above. It snakes up the side of the bath. My hand is numb – a useless lump of meat on the end of my arm.

My other hand still works, though. I slam it down on the end of the rod that switches the water from the taps to the shower, holding it firm as the water stops spurting out of the shower head and starts gushing out of the taps. It runs straight down the plughole.

Mouth open, breathing fast, I look up.

Rob's still there, but the background is clearer now – he's fading a little.

You bastard. Finish her or I'll finish you, he says.

I'm shivering but my brain has unfrozen. Get dry. I need to get dry. Leaving the taps running I climb out of the bath and start scrubbing myself furiously with a towel using the hand that still works.

I can't see Rob any more, only the place where he used to be: a slight haziness, a blurring of that space, nothing more. He's gone, or almost, but he manages one last whisper.

Finish her.

I lean against the wall, shivering, gasping. The only thing I can think is he's after Neisha. I've got to keep her safe. I've got to keep her away from the lake.

FIFTEEN

I run all the way to Neisha's house without getting a glimpse of her. Did she say she was heading home? I'm such a coward! Why did I let her go alone? The soft misty rain is still there, almost hovering in the air. I keep Mum's umbrella close to my head, avoid brushing against any wet leaves, and jump over the puddles.

The doorbell's wet. Mustn't touch it. I poke it with the handle of the umbrella and step back from the door, looking up at the windows. The front door opens. It's Neisha's dad wearing a smart polo shirt with a little logo on, tucked into his belt.

'You said an hour, Neisha. It's been—' he says as the door swings back, then sees that it's me and not his daughter standing on the doorstep. 'Oh.'

His brow is furrowed with worry and he's nervously

stroking the tufty island of hair that clings to the top of his bald head. 'Oh,' I echo. 'Hello. Is Neisha here?'

Stupid question.

'No. I was expecting her home a while ago. I thought she was visiting you, your mother ...'

'She was. She left about an hour ago.'

'So where—?'

'I don't know.'

'She should be here. Where I can keep my eye on her, take care of her. Her phone's switched off. She always switches her blessed phone off when she's with that—' He stops, like he's suddenly aware of who he's talking to. 'I'm sorry. I'm just worried. I didn't want her to go out. It's too soon, it's ... I need to know where she is.'

I'm backing away already.

'She's only sixteen. She's thinks she's an adult, that she can do what she want, go where she wants, but ...'

'I'll find her,' I say. 'I'll bring her home.'

'She knows the way home,' he says, 'but thank you.'

I run out of the gate and turn left towards the town centre. Where could she have gone? I thought she was going straight home when she left ours.

I get an idea. I don't know where she is, but I know where she mustn't be. A spasm of fear clutches at my guts. She can't be ... can she? I head towards the high street. At the top end, near the church, a lorry thunders past, spraying water up my leg. It soaks into my jeans.

Finish her.

I look round, expecting to see Rob, but the street's just full of the normal town centre types; old women with shopping trolleys, mums trailing toddlers or pushing buggies. He's not there. It was just an echo in my head. But it feels like he's just behind me, dodging out of sight when I look round.

I stumble along the pavement, half running, half walking, checking behind me every few steps.

There's a cut-through from the high street to the park, down the side of the shops. I accelerate, belting down the path. At the end, there's a bowling club, hiding behind a dense green hedge, and some tennis courts inside a high fence. Between them they cut off the view. I run between them and soon burst out into the open green of the park. There are several sets of tyre tracks in the turf running down the hill, great brown ruts gouged into the green, with water resting in the bottom. My eye follows them down and there's a figure at the base of the slope – some-one wearing a dark coat going in at the waist, long black hair trailing down her back – just disappearing through a gap in the bushes.

'Neisha!' I shout at the top of my lungs.

She turns.

'Wait! Wait for me!'

I set off down the hill, skidding and sliding but some-how staying on my feet. Water oozes around the side of my shoes with each step. Neisha watches me run and as I come clattering towards her she holds one of her arms out to the side as if she's going to catch me. I pull up before we make contact, but even so she smiles and says, 'Whoah.'

'Sorry,' I say. 'I just …'

And now I don't know what to say. How can I tell her

to stay away from the lake without sounding mad?

'Where are you going?' I ask, though I know the answer already.

The smile disappears from her face and she shrugs and looks down at the ground.

'I was just … I was going back to the … you know.'

'Going back to the lake?'

'Yeah. I thought it might help.' She's awkward, apologetic.

'No!' I say, though it comes out more like a shout.

She looks up sharply.

'It's all such a mess, Carl. It's all so horrible. I want to try and make sense of it. Or find some sort of peace or something. Sorry, that sounds lame.'

'No,' I say. 'No, it doesn't. Just … just not there, that's all. Don't go back there.'

'Someone said there were flowers there, like at your house. I wanted to see. That's all.'

'It's just flowers, Neisha. It doesn't mean anything.' There's a sulky edge to my voice and I think, I've blown it now. She's going to tell me to get stuffed.

'It's okay,' she says, putting her hand on my arm. Even through my sleeve I feel her warmth and it shocks me all over again. 'I understand if you don't want to go. It's fine. We'll go somewhere else. I can go back there on my own sometime.'

'No!'

There I go again, shouting in her face. This time a little fleck of spit jumps out of my mouth and lands near the corner of hers. Instinctively she takes her hand away from my arm and wipes the wetness away.

'For God's sake, Carl,' she says. 'What's wrong?'

'I'm sorry, I'm sorry.'

I stand uselessly before her, shoulders hunched, no idea how to stop this beautiful girl doing something that might put her in terrible danger.

She sighs. 'Let's go somewhere,' she says. 'Somewhere else.'

She slips her hand into mine and there's that warmth again. My fingers curl around hers and suddenly everything seems possible.

I can figure out what to do about Rob.

I can keep Neisha safe.

We start walking up the hill.

'Nice umbrella,' she says, and I take the hint and move it over a bit so it's covering her. My shoulder will get wet, but I'm too dazzled by her to care.

'Er ... it's Mum's.'

Wrong way, Cee.

The voice is here. Rob is here, somewhere. Watching. Wanting us to turn back towards the lake. A chill touches my neck, cold air raising the hairs. I jerk the umbrella back towards me.

'What are you—? Oh, you're getting wet. Come here.'

She lets go of my hand and moves closer to me, putting her arm round my waist.

You're dead, you bastard. You're both dead.

I stiffen. What will he do next? How can I keep her safe? I peer behind us, expecting to see Rob's pale face at my shoulder.

'It's all right,' Neisha says. 'No one's looking. Anyway we're not doing anything wrong.'

That's what she thinks. But I want my brother's girl. I want her so badly every cell in my body is aware of her closeness. My neck was cold a moment ago. Now there's blood flushing into it and up to my face. It's surging so hard into my groin I can hardly walk. I fancy my dead brother's girlfriend. How messed up is that? He's right to want me dead.

'I miss this,' she says. 'Being close to someone.'

I've never had it. Have I? Any closeness me and Rob had was a different sort of contact. Holding each other in a wrestling grip, struggling to get the upper hand. This is different. This is comfort.

And it could be more, so much more. It wouldn't take much. She could turn or I could and then we'd be face to face. My face near her face. My face touching hers …

' … to go?'

She's looking at me as if she expects an answer, and I've got no idea what she just said. I look at her blankly.

'Shall we try the coffee shop in the high street?' she says. 'The new one?'

'I dunno. Your dad's expecting you home.'

'My dad? When did you—?'

'I called round there first. He was a bit antsy …'

She rolls her eyes towards the sky.

'I'll ring him,' she says.

She disentangles herself from me, then takes her phone out of her bag and switches it on.

'Dad? I'm in the park. No, I'm fine. Honestly. I'm with

a friend, we're going to … Yes, Rob's brother. Dad, don't be like that. We're going for a coffee, okay?' She holds the phone away from her ear for a few seconds, then quickly says, 'I'll see you later,' and finishes the call.

'He's fussing,' she says.

'Can't blame him,' I say.

'I know, he never liked me going out. Now … well, now he doesn't want me to leave the house at all.'

'At least he cares,' I say.

'Yeah, I know.' The phone's ringing. She checks the screen, pulls a face, presses the off button and puts it in her bag.

'So where shall we go? High street?'

I don't want to be around people. I want it to be just me and her, like it is now. We're walking past the park café now – a bedraggled collection of plastic tables and chairs huddled on a square of concrete by a hut with a serving hatch. There are a couple of smokers sitting at one of the tables, hardened nicotine addicts who would still be out here even if it was snowing. And that's all. No one else.

'What about here?' I say.

'Whatever,' Neisha says easily. She catches my eye. 'What do you want? You hungry?'

I shake my head and we're both smiling. It feels familiar, as if we've shared secret smiles before.

We go up to the hatch and order a couple of drinks: Coke for me, coffee for her. I don't want to give up the umbrella and I don't have enough money to pay for both drinks, so I stand awkwardly for a moment until Neisha pays and picks them up. We walk over to a table, the furthest one from the smokers. The canopy in the middle is standing at an angle and one edge is hanging over the table, dripping on to it.

'Not here,' I say. 'It's wet.'

'Everywhere's wet,' Neisha says. 'Don't be soft. I'll get some serviettes.'

She puts the drinks down, wipes the table and sits down. I push at the stem of the canopy, trying to get it to stand up straight, sending a shower of drops on to Neisha, the table and me. The pole settles back down at the same angle.

Bring her to me.

'Shut up!' It's out before I can stop it.

Neisha frowns at me.

'I didn't say anything. What the hell's wrong with you?'

I feel stupid, caught out. To hide my embarrassment I crack open my can and, still standing, I sip my Coke. The sharp fizz doesn't soothe me this time. The bubbles crackling on my tongue add to my agitation.

'Sit down, Carl,' Neisha says. 'Sit down and talk to me.'

Maybe this wasn't such a good idea. Suddenly I don't want to be sitting here, surrounded by drips and drops, a soggy world holding voices, smells, things I don't want to see. I want to be inside, somewhere warm and dry. I want to sit under one of those hand dryers you get in public toilets. Sit there and feel the hot, dry air blasting over me. I want to feel safe.

But Neisha's looking at me, expecting me to sit. I pull a chair back a little and perch on the edge.

' ... early days, after all.'

I'm doing it again. Not listening.

'Carl?'

'What? Sorry. Sorry, Neisha.' My leg is jiggling ten to the dozen. I keep flipping the metal tab on the top of my can up and down, up and down. Gotta keep her safe. Gotta keep him away from ...

'You don't really want to be here with me, do you?'

'Yeah, of course I do. You're the only person ... the only one who can understand.'

'I know. That's what I've been thinking. We were the only ones there. We've been through something huge. Do you think we'll always be ... close?'

Close. Her lips touching mine. Her breath on my skin. But we can't be really close if she doesn't know what I'm going through. If I don't tell her the truth.

''Course,' I say.

It's stopped raining. Rob's gone. I relax a bit.

'Neisha,' I say. 'You know how I helped you ...'

'Yeah,' she says. 'You did more than help me. You saved my life.'

She's looking at me from underneath her eyelashes. They're thick and dark and stubby, and I wonder what it would feel like to brush the end of them with my fingertip.

'Well, I want to keep doing that. I want to keep you safe.'

Her eyes soften. She reaches across to me now, touches my wrist, and it changes everything, chasing away all thoughts of confession. She keeps her hand there, but her face darkens.

'Thanks, Carl, but there's no such thing as safe, really, is there?' she says. 'We're just hanging by a thread. One thing, just one little thing, can finish it all.'

'Like water,' I say. 'Water in your lungs, not air.' And shivers run up and down my spine, making my arms twitch. Neisha notices and her hand tightens a little. Steadying. Reassuring.

'Yes,' she says. 'Or one cell going wrong. Growing too fast, taking over.'

We're not talking about Rob any more. I'm guessing it's someone close, but I don't want to assume, say the wrong thing, spoil this.

'Like ... cancer?' I say.

'My mum,' she says and the fingers on my wrist tense further. One of her fingernails moves against my skin, digging in. I don't mind. She can give me some of her pain.

'I'm sorry,' I say. Doing that thing – apologising for something I didn't do. Understanding it now. That it's shorthand for 'I'm sorry this has happened to you'.

'Not your fault,' she says. 'Not anybody's.'

'Was it—? I mean, how long—?'

'Ages ago, when I was five. Dad moved here to make a new start. He transferred from the factory in Birmingham to the one here. S'pose he thought he was doing the right thing ...'

'Wasn't he?'

She sticks her bottom lip out a little.

'No family. No friends. Years of having no one to talk to, being the only Asian girl in the room, the only one in the whole miserable town. I love my dad, but I hated him for bringing us here.'

And if she hadn't been here, then she wouldn't have met Rob. And he wouldn't have hurt her and she wouldn't have tried to get away …

'Now this factory's closing, so God knows what we'll do next.'

Her face is so sad, not teary sad, just resigned, worn down. I want to prove her wrong. I want to make things okay. But what can I do? What can I possibly do that would make things better?

Without thinking I half rise from my chair, lean across the table and kiss her lightly on the cheek. I close my eyes and inhale as my lips brush her skin. And my head is full of white chocolate, vanilla, peaches. She's sunshine, not the feeble, half-hearted stuff we get in England – full-on, tropical sunshine.

I realise what I've just done and move slowly away from her. I hardly dare open my eyes. When I do, my self-defence mechanisms kick in. I smack my head and grin stupidly.

'Sorry, sorry. Don't know what I was doing. God, why did I do that?'

I squint at her out of the corner of my eyes, and she's smiling too.

'It's all right,' she says. 'It's all right.'

And just in this moment, in this glorious second, a fraction of time shared by us, known only to us, I feel happy. Everything else is forgotten. And I want it to stay like this for ever. I want to keep her looking at me, through her ridiculously thick eyelashes. I want to keep that light in her eyes, these dimples either side of her mouth.

There's a loud crack. Out of nowhere a gust of wind blasts under the table umbrella, stressing the fabric to bursting point. All the water gathered on top cascades on to Neisha, almost like someone is tipping over a bucket. The serviettes on our table blow on to the grass, the table itself rocks as the umbrella pole strains to escape from the hole in the middle. Neisha's coffee cup rolls on its side and dumps its contents in her lap.

Neisha screams.

She jumps up and flaps her hands as if that will shake the water away. She's dancing on the spot, squealing. Her hair is flattened against her scalp by the water from above. The top of her legs is steaming as the coffee soaks into her jeans.

I grab a handful of serviettes from the next table and hold them out towards her.

'Are you all right? Are you burnt?'

The noise she's making is halfway between laughing and crying.

After a couple of minutes dabbing at her hair and face and neck and legs, she's calmed down enough to laugh about it. The woman in the café brings her another coffee, on the house, and a towel. Neisha dries herself properly, wipes the chair again and sits down. The sun appears from behind the clouds and I can feel its warmth on my skin.

'Jesus Christ, what just happened? That was like an act of God or something!'

Despite the sunshine, her words send a shiver down my spine. In a way I'm sure she's right. It was deliberate. Someone made it happen. Someone in a jealous rage. And it reminds me how real all this is. Rob. He's still here. He wants Neisha dead.

I thought I could keep her safe, but maybe I can't.

'Neisha,' I say. 'Don't go down to the lake. Will you promise me?'

She tips her head on one side. 'I just think it's something I've got to do.'

'Not today, then. And don't go on your own. Take me with you. Promise me you won't go on your own.'

'Okay,' she says, 'I promise.'

She sips her coffee. I wish I had coffee not Coke now. I don't even like the stuff, but I want to taste the same thing as her.

'I'd better be getting back, before Dad goes completely apeshit,' she says after a while.

Without the rain, there's no excuse to huddle together, and we walk out of the park side by side, not quite touching. When our fingers accidentally bump, I look the other way, embarrassed. I'm itching to put my arm round her, draw her close, to walk in step with her, find the same rhythm. But I can't ... and I don't need to. Her fingers find mine, threading in between so our hands join up like a zip. And now I do look at her, just a glance. She's face-forward, acting cool, like she holds hands with boys all the time. But the last boy she held hands with was Rob.

I push this thought to the back of my mind and

concentrate on savouring every step between the park and her house.

Without the rain, without Rob, I feel different. Like a weight's been lifted off my shoulders. I can almost pretend that none of the other stuff is happening. None of it's real. Maybe I'm not in a nightmare, a horror story. Maybe I'm in the sort of story where something terrible happens and then the boy gets the girl. This boy gets this girl. Carl gets Neisha.

At the corner of her road, before we're in sight of her house, she unlinks her hand from mine.

'Thanks,' she says, 'for walking me home.'

'That's okay.'

'Better get in.'

'Yeah.'

'You seem better. Calmer.'

'It's you. Being with you. Talking, you know … ' and it is. Her warmth has chased away my demons. If only I could keep her with me.

SIXTEEN

Neisha. Her eyes. Her skin. Her smell. Her taste.

She's at her house and I'm walking home, but she fills my senses, and the memories come flooding back. I fancied her the first time I saw her. I wanted her when she was with Rob. But that was nothing compared to how I feel now.

I kissed her.

And she didn't shout at me, or slap me.

She held my hand.

Under my feet, there's concrete and tarmac, gravel and grass, but really I'm walking on air. Life's an unholy mess, but something good's coming out of this. Something unbelievably, wonderfully good. I want to hold on to this feeling, but of course I can't. A floodgate has opened in my mind – I'm being bombarded with memories, a tsunami of pictures and voices, tumbling over and over until one of them sticks. Me and her. Neisha and me.

And Rob.

I stop walking, lean against a wall, cover my face and watch the movie show in my head.

'Do you love her?'

He laughs.

''Course not.'

'So let her go.'

'So you can have her? I'd rather kill her.'

'Don't be stupid.'

'You're the stupid one, stupid. Do you think she'd want you, once she's seen your tiny little excuse for a dick?'

'Shut up. Just shut up.'

'She'll put down her magnifying glass, piss herself laughing and that will be that. End of.'

'Shut up. She's not like that.'

'She's exactly like that. They all are.'

'Not.'

'And you know, do you?'

He saw us, sitting in the park together, that's why he's in this rage. Well, I'm not taking it this time. I'm fighting back.

'She likes me. She kissed me. She—'

'What?'

'She kissed me and I kissed her back and she liked it.'

'You're lying. And if I ever thought you was messing behind my back, I'd kill you — both of you.'

I was lying then, though I so wanted it to be true. And now I remember how he slammed his fist into the door and then into my face. He was so angry he couldn't help

134

himself. I did that; I wound him up, made him angry.

The pieces in the jigsaw are starting to settle into place. His beatings led her to confide in me. My lie about kissing her sent him into a fury ...

So much has come back to me now. Have I remembered everything? Is this all there is to know?

I lied about it before, but this time it's real.

I start walking again. I'm back on the high street now, and as I walk past the sweet shop, hot air wafts out bringing the soft scent of vanilla. It says 'Neisha' to me, and I know it's a sign. This is it, my future – warmth and sweetness. I've earned it. I saved her. But she's still in danger. In my churning guts I know I'm going to have to save her all over again.

There are voices in the kitchen when I get home. I pop my head round the door and I'm met with a great, whooping shriek. A woman who looks like an older, fatter version of Mum gets to her feet and advances towards me, shrieking.

'It's never you. It never is. Oh my Gawd. Carl! Carl!'

She wraps her arms round me, holding a mug in one hand and a cigarette in the other. Close to, she smells like a pub ashtray.

'I'm so sorry, so sorry, sho shorry.' She's talking into my neck now. I look over her shoulder towards Mum. Her eyes are red and glassy; she's been crying. And drinking. It's not coffee in their mugs.

'You remember your Auntie Debbie, don't you?' she says. And I do. Family Christmases from when we were little; her and mum best friends on the sherry before lunch, having a laugh on white wine during the meal, fighting like alley cats on Tia Maria by the time *The Queen's Speech* is on.

'For God's sake, Debs, give him some air. You're nearly throttling him.'

Debbie unwinds herself and takes a step back.

'Let me look at you. Oh my Gawd, you look like your brother. Oh my Gawd, what a thing to happen.' Tears spill out and trickle down her face. She wipes them away with the back of her hand then strokes my face, the thumb of her cigarette hand tracing my cheekbone. The smoke makes my eyes smart and I start to cough.

'Here, let me get you some water.' Through my coughing I hear her going over to the sink, running the tap. Then she's back in my face again, thrusting a mug of water at me, holding it up to my face like I was a toddler.

'Here, here, have some of this.' She slops some into my face.

Have it. Swallow it. Breathe it. Rob's here, whispering, goading me. And it's not tap water, it's the vile stuff from the bottom of the lake – cold and rank. It's trying to choke me, get inside me, in my throat, in my lungs.

'No!'

I dash the mug from her hand and it flies across the room and smashes against a wall.

'Carl, what are you doing?' Mum's screaming at me. Debbie's screaming too.

'I was only trying to help! He's gone mad, Kerry. What's wrong with him?'

'Shuttup! Shuttup! You don't understand!' I blunder out of the room, stagger upstairs and shut myself in my room, but not before I've heard Debbie say, 'Wild animals, Kerry. Just like you said! You said they were wild animals and I didn't believe you ...'

The musty smell in the room is stronger than ever. I lie flat on my mattress, trying to calm down. Everything's all right, I tell myself. Neisha likes you. You kissed her, remember? It's going to be okay.

But it's not okay.

The stain on the ceiling is bigger, darker. It's spreading down the walls, like fingers stretching out, reaching towards me. I can feel Rob's presence ... he's here in the dampness, hanging in the air.

You always wanted her, didn't you?

It's not real, is it?

She deserves this. You both do.

I put my hands over my ears and turn over on my side, bringing my knees up to my chest.

'Stop it! Stop it!'

I'll kill you, Cee. See if I don't ...

'Just stop it, all right? I'm not listening. Leave me alone.'

There's a hand on my back. He's here. I can feel him. I don't want to look. I don't want him here, I can't bear it. I raise my arm up and swipe it behind me. My hand slams into warm flesh and there are two screams, one close, one further away. I look over my shoulder and Mum's on her arse on the floor, gaping like a fish. Auntie Debbie's standing in the doorway.

Mixed up with their screams is another sound: laughter, bouncing off the walls, rattling round the inside of my skull.

SEVENTEEN

I'm on my feet now and I'm throwing myself down the stairs, heading for the door.

'He's gone mad, Kerry. He's not safe ...'

I run out of the front and through the yard, vault over the wall and I'm gone. I don't know where I'm running to, but I can't stay in that place another minute. I run blindly through the alleys and paths, past back-garden fences and garages and bins. I want to run for ever, but my tank is nearly empty before I even begin. I slow to a jog and then start walking. My throat's dry and my legs are like lead.

I'm round the back of the school, near a set of ramshackle buildings known as The Sheds where the caretakers run their own little empire. It's the middle of Saturday afternoon now. School's empty. No staff. No kids.

I duck through a gap in the chain-link fence and I'm in. The huts themselves are locked but there's a kind of porch outside one of them with two canvas chairs set up. I sit in one of them and try to get things straight in my head.

I'm sorry I hit Mum. If it was just me and her, I could go back home and apologise. Maybe she'd hit me back, maybe she wouldn't. Whatever. I could take it. And I've got a feeling we'd be all right. We've been starting to get on. But now Debbie's there, it's different. She'll be twittering on and on, winding her up. I can't go home. Not now, not yet.

The thing is, I know what this is about now. Why Rob's so angry. He's jealous of me and Neisha, angry at me for protecting her from him. He wants Neisha dead. And he wants to make me pay by killing her. He thinks I owe him my loyalty. Well, I'm not doing it. No way. She's beautiful and kind, and I'm starting to feel like she could be my girl. It's the best feeling ever. I'm not going to let him take it away.

I've got to find a way to tell him that. What can he do, after all? He's dead, isn't he?

I sit back in the chair and close my eyes. And it's him that I see. His pale face, the zip going up and over it. And I know in the pit of my stomach that he will hurt me if I refuse him. He's in the water and water is everywhere and it feels like he can use it against me. And seeing him, hearing him, smelling him — every day, over and over — is tipping me closer and closer to madness. I hit Mum. What else will I do?

I've got to get rid of him.

Something starts buzzing in my pocket, then a ring-tone blares out. Rob's phone. For a crazy moment I think it's him. I bring it out of my pocket, but I'm too scared to look. Then I realise how stupid I'm being. I look at the screen. Neisha.

'Carl, where are you?' Her voice is small; she sounds miles away.

'I'm round the back of my school. Where are you?'

'The end of my road. I had to get out, get away for a bit.'

'What's happened?'

'I'll tell you when I see you. Can I see you?'

''Course.'

She doesn't go to this school, she goes to the one on the other side of town; blazers and ties and 'yes sir, no sir.' I tell her how to find The Sheds and set out to meet her halfway.

I see her before she sees me, and my stomach goes soft again. Walking on her own she looks so vulnerable. More than ever, more than anything, I want to keep her safe. When she spots me, she looks away and wipes her face with her sleeve. As I get close I see that her mouth is twitching – she's trying not to cry.

'Neisha, what is it?'

'Not here. Not in the street,' she says. We turn in silence and head towards the school. Our hands meet and again I get the shock of her warmth, radiating up my arm. Despite everything, it gives me a surge of hope.

I lead her through the gap in the fence into the school grounds. Now we're away from view, her shoulders start shaking and I step forward and put my arms round her. She leans her head on my shoulder and it's several minutes before she speaks.

'Everything's so bad, so wrong.'

'Has something else happened?'

'My dad … he says we're going to move back to Brum when the factory goes.'

It feels like the ground's opening up and swallowing us. She can't move. I can't lose her. Not now. I hold her tighter and stroke her hair and savour the feeling of her hands on my waist.

'He went ballistic just now, because I was out for longer than I said, because I was out with—'

'—with me.'

'Yeah. He hated Rob. Now he's saying this place is toxic, that we should never have come here …'

Her body's shaking again. I kiss the top of her head, her temple, her cheek. She's warm, so warm. She moves a little, tipping her face towards mine, and I find her lips. They're soft and wet and taste of salt tears. I press my mouth against hers gently, ready to pull back at the first hint of rejection, but after a second or two she responds to me, angling her head a little more, kissing me back. I open my mouth and she mirrors me and we take each other in – my top lip in her mouth, her bottom lip in mine. It's full and fleshy and wet and warm, and I'm melting inside, meltingly hot inside and out.

After a while, we move apart. My legs are trembling, there's sweat pooling between my shoulder blades, under my arms. 'I need to sit down,' I say, and collapse into one of the tattered canvas chairs Neisha makes to go and sit in the other one, but I pull her towards me and draw her on to my lap. I need her warmth again, and her mouth on mine. The chair creaks beneath us. Neisha pulls a face.

'Is this all right?' she says.

'Yeah,' I say. 'Everything's all right.' And now we're kissing again and one of her hands is on the back of my neck and the other is buried in my hair. When we come up for breath, we're both flushed, happy, almost shy with each other. She rests her face against mine and we sit quietly.

'Your dad was right about Rob. He still is. Neisha—'

I'm on the edge of telling her, but I hesitate, trying to find the right words. She puts her index finger up to my lips.

'He was right about Rob, but he's wrong about you ...'

And she leans close and we're kissing again. And again. And again.

There's a chill in the air. I want to stay here for ever, but it's going to be too cold soon.

'We need to find somewhere inside,' I say, thinking I could try forcing the lock on one of the huts.

'Okay,' she says, 'show me your school.' There's a sparkle in her eyes now, a glint of devilment.

'Break in?'

'Why not? I want to know all about you. The places you go. The people you know. Show me.'

We struggle to our feet, muscles stiff from being squashed into the chair. Holding hands, we walk past prefab classrooms towards the heart of the school – the main building with the hall, the canteen, the library, the staff room and the Head's office.

The windows are old metal-framed things, each pane criss-crossed into hundreds of little lozenges. Easy to slide a knife in and flick the catch ... and, of course, I've got a knife ...

We slope around to the back of the building, away from the road, away from prying eyes. The library windows are low down and out of anyone's view. I set to work. I've seen Rob do this many times. It was always his job to get in, not mine; I was just the lookout. He even knew how to disable alarms, not that he often needed to here with the caretaker being so slack.

Peering through the glass I can see that the catch at the side isn't even in place, so it's only the bottom one that's keeping it shut at all. I wiggle the blade in and poke at the metal arm until I dislodge it. I grip the edge of the frame with the tips of my fingers and pull until it comes free and the window swings out towards me. There's no alarm, as usual. We're in.

I look at Neisha. She's got her lips pressed tight together, eyes bright with excitement now, not tears.

'Shall we do it?' I ask.

'Yes,' she says. 'Give me a boost up.'

I put my hands on her waist and lift her up. She gets her feet on the window ledge, then steps on to a desk on the other side and jumps down. I follow.

The library's got that smell, it's not like anywhere else in the world. Books and dust, the polish they use on the wooden floor. It brings me back to the first time I walked in here. A whole room just for books – it boggled my mind. I liked coming here, taking a book off the shelves at random and seeing what was in it. Rob never saw the point in reading, but when he left just before his exams I came all the time. That's how it will be now, if I want it. If I ever come back to school.

Neisha's halfway to the door already. I hang back, run my fingers along the top of a row of books, enjoying the contrast of plastic-coated covers and worn soft pages ... wondering which one to pull out, what's inside.

'Come on,' she hisses, and even that sounds too loud in this empty space. 'What are you doing?'

'Nothing. Just ... nothing. I like this place, that's all. It's special. So many books.'

She shrugs. 'We've got loads of books at home.' A house full of books, like Harry's. A different sort of house to mine. 'You should have a look, borrow some.' She walks back to me and takes my hand. 'When my dad's out,' she adds. 'Come on.'

We walk into the corridor. It's eerie without anyone else here. Our trainers squeak on the smooth tiles of the floor. I want to like it, being here, to feel like The Man, breaking in, bringing my girl here, but I just feel small. The emptiness reminds me of all the people missing, of Rob, who used to fill these halls, but won't ever be here again.

I start looking for something to chase this feeling away. I want to impress Neisha, hear her laughter echoing off the blank walls.

There's nothing in the school hall. Everything's been tidied away – it's just a big empty space. There's an air of boredom still clinging to the place, though. Nothing can get rid of that. Hundreds of kids packed in here day after day for assembly, sitting in rows on hard plastic chairs. Numb backsides, numb brains. Breathing in each other's farts.

I lead her out of the hall and we find the corridor by the Head's office. I try the door; it's locked. There are three chairs outside; the place where you wait to be summoned. Death row.

'Here,' I say and I sit down, pulling her down next to me. I fish in my jacket pocket and pull out the cigarette packet and matches. 'Do you fancy a ciggie?'

I spark up a match and hold it carefully for Neisha. She draws her cigarette into life, takes a long drag and then blows the smoke towards the ceiling.

'Aren't you having one?'

I remember the last time I tried, choking on the harsh smoke.

'Nah,' I say, aware I'm probably losing cool points.

I flick the match towards the bin beside my chair, then strike another one and flick that too. Neisha watches with approval as she smokes.

'Bet you've sat here plenty of times,' she says.

And I have. And I can remember, just like that. I don't even have to try.

I remember what it was like waiting for my turn to go in. Sitting forward in my chair, keeping my eyes down, watching people's legs as they walked past. And Rob next to me, sitting back, head against the wall, making eye contact with everyone. Telling them all, *Yeah, I'm here again. So what?* with every glance.

Is everything back now? Have I remembered it all?

'Yeah. They don't do anything though,' I say. 'Give you a bollocking. Suspend you. It's nothing, is it? What's your school like?'

She opens her mouth to reply, then stops. She looks past me. There's smoke wisping out of the bin, and now an actual flame licking the balled-up paper inside.

'Oops,' she says, then catches my eye and laughs.

'Better put it out,' I say, looking round for a cloth or an extinguisher or something, but before I can find anything there's a noise so loud, so piercing that it sets all the little bones in my ears rattling. At the same time it starts raining. Not pattering on the roof or the windows, but raining *inside* — spraying out from the ceiling, pissing on to the floor.

Neisha starts squealing. She's laughing at the same time.

'Oh my God! Look at it!'

She spins around in the middle of the corridor, holding her hands out, catching the drops on her palms, on her face. Then she stops for a moment and looks at me.

I'm not laughing.

The water rains down on me and almost instantly he appears. Rob. He's in the corridor behind Neisha. Cold hate radiates from him as he looks first at me, then her. The black holes where his eyes should be burn with a dark fire.

'This is crazy! It's crazy, isn't it?' Neisha shouts at me. 'Carl?'

'We've got to get out of here, Neisha. We've got to get out now!'

EIGHTEEN

She's soaking, her long hair hanging in rats' tails around her shoulders. Now she's starting to shiver.

'Okay, okay. It's just water. Bloody freezing, though!'

'No, you don't understand. Just run, Neisha. Get out of here.'

She turns and starts running away from me, her feet making a slapping noise on the wet floor. She's going to run straight into him.

'No! Stop!' I don't know which of them I'm shouting at, but Neisha turns to glance back at me and slows down. Behind her, Rob's face is immobile, set in a grim death mask.

'Not that way!'

'I'm getting soaked, Carl! I've gotta get out of here.'

'But he's here. He's right here.'

She turns her confused face to me and now they're lined up: her in front, him behind. He's still standing there – silent, staring.

'Who's here? What are you on about?'

She's so close to him. He could reach out and touch her ...

'Rob,' I say.

She wheels round, then turns back again.

'There's no one ...'

'He's right behind you, Neisha. Come back this way.' I beckon to her with both hands. Her face is still question-ing me, but she moves towards me, slowly. Behind her, Rob moves too.

The water's still spraying out from the ceiling. My clothes are saturated. It's dripping off my hair, my nose, everywhere. The alarm's blaring out, rattling my head. And he's coming for us.

Neisha's close now. 'There's no one here, Carl,' she says, trying to soothe me. There's no time to explain. As she reaches her hand up to stroke my hair, I grab it and start pulling her along the corridor, away from Rob.

'What are you—? What's going on?'

The water is starting to pool on the floor, there's nowhere for it to go. It's beginning to rise up the bottom of the tiled walls. And it's not clean, it's brown and foul.

'Come on. Come on!' I shout. 'We've got to get out of here!'

I yank at her hand again and she starts to run with me. The water's coming down so fast it's almost ankle deep now. We run to the end of the corridor and Neisha slips on the wet tiles. It's so sudden, I can't keep hold of her. She's down before I know it. For a moment she lies there, flat on her front, face down in the water.

Frozen and horrified, I stare at her. A small wave washes over the back of her head. A layer of water that seems to cradle the curve of her neck, forming fingers that are pressing her down, forcing her face under.

She's drowning.

Yesss! Rob's triumphant voice hisses in my ear.

'No!' I yell.

I reach down and pull her head and shoulders out of the water. There's an awful moment when she doesn't react. Her face is blank, her body limp in my hands. Then she retches, violently and again, until at last her throat is clear and she's breathing properly again. Her hands grip my arms and I pull her on to her feet.

'Shit!' she gasps, wiping the water from her hands and mouth.

'You okay?'

'Yeah. Maybe. I hate my face in the water. It's like ... it's just like ...'

'I know,' I say, realising that in those few seconds she was back in the lake, out of her depth, fighting for her life. This time it was only a few centimetres deep, but it nearly had her.

I want to hug her, there and then. Hold on tight and never let her go. But the water's still falling, the alarm's still ringing, and Rob's still here somewhere. 'Come on,' I say. We need to get away, get out of here, get dry before he comes for us again.

Around the corner there are a couple of steps. We stagger up and I notice the difference at once: the floor's dry. The sprinklers aren't going in this section of the building. We're both still drenched. We leave wet footprints as we run along together.

Rob's still with us. Behind one moment, in front the next. He's yelling at me.

You fucking traitor.

'How are we going to get out?' Neisha asks.

I'm getting stronger, little brother.

'We'll try another window. Here—'

Help me kill her ...

In a panic I push against the metal plate on the next door to the left. The door swings open and we bundle inside. It's the girls' toilets.

The door swings to behind us, rocking on its hinges until it settles, and Neisha and I look at each other. The alarm is fainter in here but now we can hear a siren, maybe two, coming from outside.

'Fire engines,' I say. 'Police too, probably.'

... or I'll kill you both.

I turn round and yank at the roller towel on the wall behind the door. It's the sort that pulls out a little way before feeding back up into the metal box. I duck down and scrub at my wet hair, rubbing my ears to try and get all the water out. Get him out, away from me, away from her.

'Get the other towel,' I say to Neisha. 'Try and get dry.'

'It's all right. I'll do it when I get home. I just want to get out of here,' she says.

There's a row of four cubicles in the room, and we're

standing by a couple of basins. They've got mirrors on the walls above them and further up the wall, two little windows with frosted glass. The windows are pretty small.

'What do you reckon?' I say, looking up.

'No, Carl. Let's go back. There must be an easier way.'

'There isn't, Neisha, not without getting soaked again, and the cops will be here any minute. Trust me. I need to get you out of here. There's a little yard the other side with some benches and that. You might be able to drop on to one of them – it's not so far down. Here, I'll help you up.'

She puts one foot up on to the edge of a sink and I give her a boost. I hold her legs steady as she unhooks the catch on the window and pushes it open. The tap at the sink is dripping.

'I don't know …' she says.

'Step on to the taps, then pull yourself up.'

She checks back at me. I nod at her encouragingly, even though I'm not sure if she can make it and I'm certain that I can't. She puts one foot on top of the cold tap. Her foot must have moved it, because the dripping's turned into a stream. Then I realise the other tap at this sink is going too. And both the ones at the second sink. I shiver.

'Go, Neisha. Go. Go now.'

The water isn't draining away. It's rising up the sides, and it's brown. It fills my nostrils with the smell of decay. I turn the taps, all of them, but it doesn't make any difference. The water's still coming.

'Neisha, quickly.'

'I think I can do it,' she calls back, 'but what about you?'

'I'll be fine. I'll get out somewhere else.'

'I'm not going without you,' she says.

The brown water is up to the brim, spilling out on to the floor.

'You've got to. Your dad'll go mental if they take you down the cop shop, you know he will. You go, Neisha. Go now.'

'Okay,' she says, 'okay, but call me when you're home, will you?'

'Yes, I'll call you.'

'Promise?'

'Yes. Now please, please go!'

She gives a little jump and pulls her head and shoulders through the gap.

To my right, there's a mechanical thunk, the groan of metal on metal and the sound of tumbling, swirling water. What's happening?

Neisha's still struggling to ease herself through the window. She hasn't heard the noise, but my blood's running cold.

She's halfway out now, wriggling through the hole and for a terrible moment I think she's stuck. I can see her hands on the other side of the window, pressing against the frosted glass. And now her legs slither through and her feet disappear. There's a thump and she gives a little cry.

I clamber up on to the sink and cram my face up to the window.

'Are you okay?'

She's picking herself up off the ground.

'Yeah,' she says. 'Can you get out?'

'I'll be all right. Just get out of here, Neisha. Go. Now.'

Outside the air is cold and clean and dry. It's starting to get dark. Behind me I hear pipes knocking and banging from within the row of toilets, water cascading on to the floor. I've got the rank smell of it in my nose, it's stinging my eyes.

I watch Neisha run out of the yard. Then I jump down from the sink. My feet splash in the brown water on the floor. It's over the top of my shoes now. I take a couple of steps towards the toilets.

'Rob?' I call out. I could run out of here, run away again … but I'm dog tired, the cold is sapping my strength and, besides, I want to face him. I need to stop him, make him leave us alone.

I look along the row of closed doors. Water's coming from underneath all of them. I walk up to the first one and push it gently. I hold my breath as the door moves under my fingers, swinging back on its hinges. The cubicle's empty and I can see that the water is flowing in from the one next door.

I breathe out and step back again.

I steel my nerve to try the second door. Same thing.

I move back from the door and lean against the wall. Two doors left.

The knocking noise is louder. It's coming from the cubicle at the end. I move to face the door. He's in there. He must be.

There's a gap between the bottom of the door and the surface of the water that's coming out. Holding my breath, I crouch down and turn my head sideways to peer through. I wobble a little as I crane forward, and put my hand down to steady myself. The stinking brown water ripples against my fingers, and the cold is so intense it feels like the water is grabbing me, holding on, pulling me. I glance down, expecting to see the watery fingers that were pressing on Neisha's neck wrapping themselves around my wrist, digging in, tugging.

There's a loud bang, the sound of splintering. The door bursts open and a wall of water comes towards me, a fountain of thick, frothing stuff pluming out of the toilet bowl and crashing on to the floor in a tidal wave of filth.

I'm screaming now as I rock back and slam into the wall behind me. The water hits me in the face, in my eyes, my nose, my mouth. My scream is extinguished, snuffed out as the water forces its way into my throat.

I've got to get out of here, get out now, or I'll die.

Coughing and choking, I scrabble past the other cubicles on my hands and knees. I don't care any more what my hands are touching, what my feet are wading through. I've just got to get out of here.

On my feet now, I blast through the door and hurtle down the corridor.

You fucking let her go.

Suddenly he's in front of me, standing square in the middle of the corridor.

I skid to a halt.

You had my girlfriend, you killed me. You owe me!

I lurch round and head back the other way. Soon I'm at the steps, the flooded corridor where this all started. The water is covering the first step. The sprinklers are still going. I feel each drop as it hits my skin. The water by my feet slows me down. The water from above reminds me of that other time, the time in the lake.

The sky's so dark above me. A curtain of rain surrounds me and now I can't see. I twist and turn but it's the same in every direction. Water above me, around me, below me. It's in my eyes, my ears, my mouth. It's pushing out everything else. I can't breathe. I can't breathe. I can't …

The water is flowing into my mouth. I swallow and taste mud. It churns in my stomach, writhing, trying to force its way back up again.

He's here, standing a couple of metres away. He leans forward and foul stuff pours out of him, tipping into the water at my ankles, and I can feel it rising up inside me, too, the same cold, vile fluid. Every time I cough it brings it closer to my throat. I try to swallow, but my muscles spasm. I can't control it.

Kill her. Bring her to the lake.

'No way, Rob You'll have to kill me first.'

If that's what you want …

The water's inside me, I'm coughing and swallowing and it's rising. I bend over, heaving and retching, then stand with my hands on my thighs, as the water from the sprinkler rains down on me.

'Go away. Leave me alone!' I gasp.

It's your fault.

His face darkens, the gaping holes of his eyes and mouth and nose merging. The sirens are getting nearer. More than one – a string of them, speeding their way closer.

He's moving towards me and I start stepping back. Is he going to kill me? Kill me here?

I want to run again, but I'm exhausted. I take a deep breath but it catches in my throat, and I'm coughing again.

He's close to me now and the stench of decay is making me gag. I want to turn and run so badly. I make myself stand still.

'I didn't mean to kill you. I was just getting you off her, that's all. I never meant ...'

It was your fault we were in the lake at all.

The sirens are next to the building now. Flashing lights turn the corridor into a crazy waterlogged disco.

'What?'

You told me to kill her. And kill her we will.

The urge to vomit again is getting stronger. The lights and the noise and the water and the smell are making me dizzy. And his words. What he's saying doesn't make sense ...

'That's not right. It can't be. I wouldn't ... I didn't ...'

There are other lights now. Torch beams shining from the end of the hallway, dazzling me with their glare.

'Are you all right down there? Can you hear me?'

I look directly into the light, past Rob, through him, but I can't make out the owner of the voice. I shield my eyes and when I look again, the torches have been directed to the floor and there are shadowy figures walking towards me – there one minute, gone the next, nearer each time the blue light flickers on from outside.

'Can you tell me where the fire is, son? Is it out?'

The bin's tipped over on one side, lying in the water.

I can't speak. I'm numb. It was my fault? I told him to do it?

It can't be true. I can't remember.

The lead fireman is nearly level with Rob now.

'Where's the fire, son?' he says. 'Where's the fire?'

I don't say anything. I'm watching Rob, as the guy steps through him without noticing a thing.

You. Told. Me. You. Dared. Me, he whispers.

The fireman shouts behind him, 'It's okay. All out. Turn the sprinkler off.' And then he turns and puts his hand on my arm and I let him lead me outside, and turn me over to the police.

NINETEEN

'Carl? Is that you? You sound funny.'

Neisha's on the phone. The girl Rob said I wanted dead. The girl he said I dared him to kill. The light from the screen forms a bright square in the darkness of my room.

'Yeah, it's me.'

'Are you okay? Did you get home okay?'

Her voice is low, almost a whisper. I picture her talking in the dark, in the midnight hush of her house.

'Look, I can't talk right now.'

Not with this ball of guilt lodged in my throat. Not when I don't know what to say to her, whether to tell her or to carry on with what could be a big, fat lie inside me. The lie that I'm her hero.

'Is there someone there?'

'No, it's just …'

'Please, Carl, I need to talk to someone. I need to talk to you.'

She thinks she needs me, but who am I? The boy she thinks I am, or the one Rob says I am? I want it to be the one she believes in so much. But how can I just carry on as we were?

I crawl out of my pit and take the phone downstairs into the kitchen, away from the shared wall and the stereo snoring.

'I'm worried about you, Carl. Are you okay?'

'Yeah, I'm fine. Got home via the cop shop.'

She gasps. 'Did they——? I mean, was it——?'

'Nah, it was okay. They just questioned me and brought me back here. I've got to go back again in a few days' time. They won't do anything until after the funeral.'

'Are they going to charge you?'

'Depends. If I play the dead brother card I might just get a caution.'

I can hear how cynical that sounds, but it's true. It's no worse than spinning your teacher a line about your grandma dying to explain the odd day bunking off. It's better than that: at least it's not a fib.

Neisha's quiet for a little bit, then, 'You didn't mention me?'

'I didn't say anything. Not a thing.'

'Thanks. My dad went nuts when I got home. You were right, he would have gone ballistic if the police had picked me up.'

'No need for both of us to get in trouble. I'm just glad you're safe.'

'I'm glad you're safe too. It got a little … crazy in there, didn't it? Thanks for getting me out. You're a gentleman. You know, you're nothing like your brother. I was so busy looking at him, coping with his moods, I didn't really see past him. But you were always there for me, weren't you, like you are now. When can I see you again?'

Right now? No! Don't, Carl. Don't. *I'm not who you think I am.* Oh God, oh God. I'm thinking this, but at the same time I'm blushing, soaking up the warmth that she's giving me, phone to phone, mouth to ear. Mouth. Her mouth. Oh God. This has to stop.

'I don't think it's a good idea.'

'What?' Her voice is suddenly sharp.

'Seeing each other.'

'Why? Why would you say that?'

'I just … it's just …' I'm flailing around trying to find the right words, '… it doesn't feel right. Not so soon.'

'That's why it *is* right. We've been through so much together. I need you, Carl. Don't cut me off. Not now.'

'But I don't know who I am!'

'It's okay, you're just getting your memory back, and I'm just finding out all about you, too, but what I'm finding I love. I love …'

'Don't. Don't say stuff like that. What I'm saying, what I'm trying to say, is that you think I'm this sweet boy, but maybe I'm not. Maybe I'm just like my brother.'

'No, Carl. You've always been in his shadow, but the real you is different. Trust me. I can see you for who you are. You're kind, Carl. You're sensitive.'

I wanna laugh now, laugh out loud, but I do my best to

stifle it. I wish I could believe what she's saying is true.

'You know earlier, at the school, you said you saw Rob ...'

'I was just ... confused, I dunno.'

'But you saw him, didn't you? That's what you said.'

No point denying it. 'Yeah.'

'Because you feel guilty and you miss him?'

'Maybe. You don't think I'm losing my marbles?'

'No, I don't think so. I think it's your way of expressing your grief.'

I want to believe her, to be swept along by her, live in her world. It's so hard living in mine.

'But he talks to me, Neisha.'

'What?'

'I can hear him, as well as see him. I can smell him too.'

Silence. Not a comfortable silence, a tense one. The atmosphere's changed, just like that.

'Maybe you should tell someone. A doctor or someone.'

'I don't want a doctor, Neisha. I don't need one. He's real. I swear he is.'

'That's just rubbish, Carl. When people die, they stay dead. Trust me, I know.'

And suddenly I feel a sense of relief. Her words are so blunt, so straightforward. There's no room for doubt in her mind. When people die, they stay dead. Simple. End of.

Rain starts pattering on the kitchen window and in spite of what Neisha's just said I can hardly bear to look, thinking of his pale fingers, tapping, scratching. I force myself to stand up, walk over to the sink and face the outside world. It's just rain, spit-spotting on to the glass.

A memory kicks in again,

Rain pit-patting on the leaves above me.

Crawling through bushes, peering into a clearing.

'*Did you kiss him? Did you kiss Carl?*'

No.

'*You did, didn't you? Is that why you want to finish it?*'

I hear the smack of flesh on flesh. Neisha's gasp.

'*No. And I don't want to finish it any more. I said, didn't I?*'

'*You haven't answered the question, bitch. Did you snog my brother?*'

'*No! I told you. I don't fancy Carl. I never have.*' *She laughs. '*He's ... like a brother. A teddy bear. Who wants to shag a teddy bear?*'*

I spin away, leaning against the wall, eyes stinging with humiliation.

'Carl, are you there? Are you still there, Carl?'

'Yeah. Yeah, I'm here.'

'What are you doing? Where are you?'

'It's raining, Neisha.'

'*They stay dead.*' I want it to be true. I want her to be right, I walk through into the hall to the front door, flick the catch and open it. I step out into our yard, feel the rain on my bare shoulders.

But he's there, shimmering and half-seen for a while, becoming clearer the wetter I get.

The phone's still in my hand, down by my thigh. Neisha's voice is a million miles away.

'Carl, Carl! Are you there? Can you hear me?'

'*I told you — if I thought she snogged you, I'd kill you both.*'

163

We're in our room, face to face, eyeball to eyeball.

And just for a moment, I remember her laughing about me, feel the tears stinging again and I wish I'd never seen her. I wish she'd never existed. I wish she was dead.

'I didn't touch her, okay? I don't give a shit about her. You can hit her as much as you like. Kill her for all I care, but leave me out of it.'

His eyes glitter.

'You want me to kill her? You're on, mate. You're fucking on.'

'You won't do it, Rob. You wouldn't dare. You beat people up, people smaller and weaker than you, but you're not a killer. You're all mouth. I hate you as much as I hate her.'

It's true. Everything he said is true. The last memory has slotted into place and now I know that I'm as bad as he said. I'm the monster Rob's told me I am.

I'm the person who wanted Neisha dead, who, in the heat of the moment, told Rob to do it, who persuaded Neisha to go to the lake. Okay, so I'm the one who watched and then dived in to save her too, but what does that make me? Does one good act cancel out the other?

We're in the yard together, in the dark, in the rain. Me and Rob. Rob and me.

From a million miles away, Neisha's voice reaches me. 'Carl? Carl? Who are you talking to? Who's there?'

I lift the phone up, look for the 'off' button and press.

TWENTY

'Carl, wot you doing out 'ere?'

Mum's standing in the doorway. Her face is crumpled and flushed. She's wearing an old T-shirt and nothing on her legs.

Rob looks past me, right at her.

Mum.

She can't hear him, can't see him. But can she sense something? She shivers, clutching her arms across her body.

'Iss freezin' out 'ere. For Gossake, Carl, get in. You're soaked.'

I look down. My chest is running with water. My tracksuit bottoms are drenched.

She darts out from the shelter of the porch and grabs my elbow.

I stumble backwards, still facing Rob as he mouths, *You and me. You and* …

I'm back inside and the door's firmly shut. Mum's towelling my hair dry roughly. She's got another towel wrapped round my shoulders. Rob's fading. It's only his voice now, on repeat, getting fainter.

You and me …

He's drowned out by Mum, firing questions at me.

'What were you doin' out there? Why were you up the school thissevening? What the hell's goin' on with you, Carl?'

She doesn't give me time to answer, which is fine by me.

And then she stops. She stands back, with the towel in her hands, and she looks at me. Her eyes are still red from the booze, she's not too steady on her feet, but she means business. She wants me to talk.

'So wass goin' on?'

'Nothing. Nothing's going on, Mum.'

'Don't gimme that. Why did you go mental thissafternoon and hit me? Why did you run off?'

'That was an accident. I'm sorry, okay? I thought you were …'

'Who? Debs? You thought it was all right to hit your auntie Debbie?'

'No, 'course not. I thought it was …'

'And then you go off up the school an' set fire to it! I mean, what the fuck, Carl? I thought you might have learnt something from all this. I thought you might have realised you can't keep acting like a … like a thug, but you've learnt nothin'. Nothin'!'

She's shouting now, ranting, and from upstairs a bleary voice calls down, 'You all right, Kerr? Wass goin' on?'

'Iss nothing, Debs. Go back to sleep.'

'How long's she going to be here?'

'*She? She? She* is my sister, and she can stay as long as she likes. She's here to help me. To help me get through, because I dunno how I'm gonna do it, face the next coupla days, God help me. Thass wot I need, Carl. I don't need you playin' up.'

'I'm sorry, I'm sorry, I'm sorry, I'm sorry …'

'You're just takin' the piss now. You let me down today. Big style. I wan' you to think about what I said, Carl. You can't go on like this.'

She wobbles off into the kitchen and I take the chance to escape upstairs. I close my bedroom door, but I can still hear her plodding up and into her room, as I peel off my wet joggers, and then Debbie and her picking me to pieces. I slip back into my sleeping bag and try to tune out their words, let their voices become just another sound, a background noise, but there aren't just two voices, there's a third, a low-level whisper. It doesn't take long for the booze to put them back to sleep again. Their voices get quieter and there are bigger gaps between their exchanges. And soon enough the snoring starts up again.

And the whisper is there. The third voice. And even as I strain to catch the words I recognise the tone, the rhythm, the pitch.

You and me, Carl. You and me …

I sit up and grope for the light switch, shielding my

eyes until, little by little, they can cope. The light reaches every corner of the cramped room. There's nowhere to hide. There's nothing to see. Except two mattresses, heaps of clothes, a couple of fishing rods and the damp patch in the corner. But it's not just in the corner now. It's bridged the gap between our beds, spreading to my side of the room. Its ragged edge reaching forwards, grasping, stretching. I put my hand on the wall, half a metre from the tip of the dark patch. The surface is damp, cold and clammy.

Kill the bitch.

He's here. In this room. He's never going to leave me alone.

Wherever I go, whatever I do, he'll be there.

My fingers find the fragments of photo in the pocket of my jeans on the floor. I fetch them out and hold them in the palm of my hand. There's an eye looking at me from the piece on top. Deep brown. Dancing with light. Neisha. My Neisha. And I think of those other photos, the ones on his phone.

I crawl across the floor and fish the phone out of the jacket pocket. I page through the screens – menu, gallery – to the photos. This time I'm not looking at her body, I'm looking at her face, the pain behind her eyes.

'*He hit me.*'

I go through each image in turn. Delete. Are you sure you want to delete? Yes. Until they're gone. I put the phone back in the pocket.

I would never hurt her. I would never let anyone else hurt her. Except that I did. I made everything worse – with my lies and my jealousy and my childish resentment. I wound him up and set him off. That last time, it was just a row like a million other rows. It ended the same, too, with him battering me. And I never thought ... I never imagined ...

It's got to stop. But how can I stop him?

This room is full of him. It's infected and so am I. He's wormed his way into my head. That's what he is, a worm in my brain.

It's this place – I've got to get out of here. But he'll come with me, won't he? I bring him with me. In the park, in the street, in the school.

He. Comes. With. Me.

And now I know what I've got to do. Neisha's dad is right. But it's not the place that's toxic, it's me. I've got to get out of here. Leave and take Rob with me, away from this flat and away from this town. Away from Neisha.

I've got to go. Tonight. Find a place where I've never hurt anyone, or broken anything or broken in anywhere. See if I can start again. Just me and my shadow. Me and him for ever.

You can't leave. I won't let you.

He's still here. He knows what I'm planning to do. Of course he knows. I spring away from the wall and stand up.

I said I'd fucking kill you and I will.

I scan round the room, looking for things to take with me. I pull on some pants, socks and a pair of jeans, and reach for a spare T-shirt, stuff it and a couple of pairs of pants in my coat pocket. There's room for my book, too.

It's the only thing here that's really mine. There's nothing else. No reminders or souvenirs. I just want to leave it all behind. Except for the picture. My torn-up girl.

Neisha.

How can I just leave her like this? Will I ever see her again? When I figure out how to get rid of Rob for good – maybe then I can come back.

I can ring her tomorrow, when I'm far enough away. Try and explain. She'll understand, won't she? Maybe she'll even wait for me.

I don't know, but I do know this is the right thing to do.

The wind's got up outside. It whines as it hits the corner of the flats, but I can't hear any rain. I want there to be rain. I need it on me, on my hair and my skin, in my face. As long as I'm wet I'll be able to drag Rob away with me.

I peer out through the curtains and I think, This is the last time I'll look out of here. It feels good, like I'm on the right track.

Right on cue, big fat raindrops start flicking against the glass. This is it. Time to go. I tie the coat around my waist, hesitate in the doorway and look back at the room. The stain on the wall is turning it into a dark, damp cave. If I stay here, I'll suffocate. It's time to go.

The snoring has died down to a low rumble in Mum's room. I wonder how long it will take her to realise I've gone. She's not going to be happy when I miss the funeral. I should leave a note. Something to stop them looking for me, raising the alarm. I turn back and rip a page out of an old schoolbook, then scrabble through the heaps on the floor looking for a pen or pencil.

Dear Mum.

I'm stuck. All I can think of to say after fifteen years, and I'm not even sure about the 'Dear'.

sorry I got to go. its for the best trust me. don look for me, its better for everyone if you don find me.

That should do it. I can't bring myself to write 'love' so I just put my name. *Carl Adams.* Then I feel a dick for putting the Adams and I want to screw it up and start again, but I want to get off now. I need to go.

I tiptoe downstairs and put the note on the kitchen table.

I ease the front door open, and slip out, pulling the door to very, very slowly. It gives a little click as the catch jolts into place and I'm out of here.

I get a blast of cold, wet air straight away. Jesus, I'm going to freeze without a top on, but it's got to be like this. As the rain starts spattering my bare skin, the whispering stops and Rob appears in the yard.

I start to run.

Running away?

I jog along the walkway and jump down the stairs. I look behind me to see if he's swinging over the concrete rail, but he isn't behind me. He's jumped in front, waiting, watching.

You always was a coward, little brother.

I was a coward, he's right, that's what got us into this mess. I didn't have the guts to stand up to him. But I'm not one now. Not any more. I have to be strong for Neisha.

I don't stop. I'm round the corner now and heading for the rec. The wind buffets me in the face, carrying the rain with it. I'm cold already, and my chest is aching as I suck in the stormy air, but I don't mind. I'm riding a wave of confidence. I've got a plan and it's working. For the first time in a long time, I'm in control.

Cold and soaked through, I head towards the edge of town – the railway, the factory and the fields beyond – and Rob tags along, as I knew he would.

For a while my route heads towards Neisha's. Then, instead of crossing the bridge and turning into her road, I carry on alongside the river. Even in the dark I can see that it's running high. The rain from the last few days has swollen it, and now it flows fast and strong a few centimetres below the top of the bank. It glistens in the streetlight like a big, fat snake.

When I turn away from Neisha's, Rob starts to get more agitated. His transparent form paces the pavement, shouting and cursing, arms flailing by his sides.

The wind's picking up. Leaves rise in a corkscrew in front of me, swirling round madly. The rain's coming harder now.

There's hardly anyone else around. No other pedestrians. A few cars. Traffic lights reflect on the wet surface of the road, broad bright streaks of colour that look like they've been painted there.

You can't do this, you coward!

His voice is a roar, in my face, in my ears, in my head. He's right in front of me. And I run at him and I keep running, bracing myself for the moment of contact. At the last minute I can't help closing my eyes. When I open them again he's standing ahead of me, on the bridge over the bypass.

I jog towards him. I feel exposed here. The wind's gusting from all directions, pushing and pulling at me. Below, cars stream towards us, under and away. Streaks of white light one side of the road, streaks of red on the other. I could get down the embankment, hitch a lift. But if I really want to disappear, I've got to find a way of doing it without being seen.

A lorry rumbles across the bridge, sloshing water over my feet, big wheels at touching distance. I reel back and hold on to the bridge's handrail, and then something clicks in my brain.

A lorry. They're in and out of the factory twenty-four seven.

I should be able to find a wagon and climb in the back without being spotted. There's security there, but with the weather this filthy I'm betting the guys will be in a nice warm office having a brew.

I set off towards the factory gates, open like always. I stand behind one of the brick gateposts and look into the site. There's a long drive, sweeping between two lines of trees, leading all the way to the factory. In between the trees there are streetlights, but they only throw their glow a few metres either side of the road. I leave the gateway and follow the fence round to the right.

The rain's coming in earnest now. The wind's blowing in my face – it's a struggle to make any headway. Suddenly a big gust comes in from the side, blowing me into the fence. The trees in the avenue to my left are thrashing around. There's a splintering noise and a branch lands a couple of metres away.

I won't let you do this. I'll kill you.

And I get the crazy feeling that the weather's on his side. That he might even be controlling it. The wind and rain are trying to stop me. I push off from the fence, pick my way past the branch and start running again. The cold's got to me now. My legs have lost their strength and I can't feel my fingers.

I make it to the factory buildings. I don't have time to check for CCTV, I've only got one thought in my mind. Find a lorry and get out of here. I cut down between two buildings into a yard behind. There are three lorries parked up, no one around, so I scuttle to the back and look for a way in. One of the trucks is a flatbed with canvas sides. The canvas is rippling in the wind, billowing out and pressing back, whipping and cracking under the strain. It's tied down with straps and buckles, but there's one place where it's started to get loose and is flapping at the bottom. I reach up and try to unpick the rope to make a bigger hole, but my fingers aren't working properly. I blow on them and try again. One of the knots starts to give – I scrape the skin off my finger and thumb and at last I'm able to feed the rope through.

I yank at the canvas and haul myself up on to the platform of the truck. Most of the space is dry but, just where I've got in, the rain has got in too. I flop down on to my back in the damp patch – keep wet, keep him with me. I glance across at Rob. He's sitting curled up, clutching his knees into his body. He stares at me with simmering hatred. And a cold pain stabs my head. He's going to make me suffer for taking him away.

This isn't over.

I breathe through the pain and listen to the wind battering against the canvas. He's not going to win. The lorry rocks, creaking and complaining, like a ship at sea. It's wild outside and it's going to be a long night.

My brother's with me, stabbing ice in my head, shackled to me by the puddle of water under my back. With no one else in the yard, I guess we're not going anywhere until the morning. All I can do is wait. But I've survived everything that Rob's thrown at me so far, and I'm on my way out of here. Everything's going to plan.

I sit up and put my spare T-shirt on. My jeans are still soaked and the T-shirt will get wet enough from the puddle to keep Rob with me. I untie my coat from my middle and roll it up for a pillow. I lie down again and curl up on my side, bringing my hands up to my face, cupping them to catch the warmth from my breath.

I take another look at Rob. He's huddled and silent now. For the first time in days, I don't feel threatened by him. It's me and him, like it always used to be, but now the tables have turned.

I close my eyes and before long the noise of the subsiding storm and the creeping comfort of my own body heat is lulling me towards sleep.

TWENTY-ONE

'I don't know why they're talking about closing – we're busier than ever,' a gruff voice says.

I open my eyes and try and work out where the hell I am. A shadow that looks like Rob stares back at me and for a moment I think I'm at home, we're on our parallel mattresses and it's the start of another ordinary day.

Then I remember he's dead.

'It's crazy. We're making a bloody fortune for 'em and it's still not enough,' another voice says.

I'm in a huge rectangular tent, lying in a puddle. The voices are very close, just the other side of the canvas. I lie still, listening, while the memory of finding this place in the middle of the night slowly comes back to me.

'It's greed, though, innit? They can save on wages in

Poland, so that's what they do. Here, hang on, you got trouble here—'

'What is it?'

'Straps have gone. Not surprised with that bloody wind. Is it just these ones?'

Feet make their way all round the truck.

'Yeah, it's just those two, but you can't go out like that.'

'I'll report it, see if I can take the other wagon.'

So this lorry's not going anywhere. Shit! One set of feet heads off across the yard. The other stays put. I can hear the guy playing with the straps and buckles, see the shadows his hands make on the other side of the canvas.

I ease myself on to my hands and knees. It's a painful business – my limbs are stiff and sore after a night sleeping in the cold. Crouching low, I move to the opposite side of the truck. The canvas is held in place tightly. No way out here. I creep back, slipping my arms into my coat. My jeans and T-shirt are still damp. The shadow hands have disappeared, and I can't hear anything.

I put my face down by the gap, and tug at the canvas gently until there's a slit. All I can see is someone's broad back inside blue overalls, about half a metre from me. I can't hope to slip out behind him without being heard or seen.

There's a shout from across the yard.

'We can use this one! I'll back it up.'

Blue Overall moves away to the side. When I can't see him any more, I make the gap bigger and peer out. It's okay. I turn round and slither out backwards on my belly, letting myself down slowly, feeling with my toes for somewhere to take my weight.

Once on the ground I crouch down, then scurry across the gap between my truck and the next. I remember now that the other two trucks in the yard had metal sides. I won't be able to get into them, so I'll have to do it another way. I've got a picture in my head of how they do it in the movies, clinging on to the underside of trucks and planes and trains. Looking at the bottom of this truck, I can't see that would be possible. You'd have to be Superman to hold on here.

What now? The cold pain in my head's back, a searing ache that threatens to dull my thinking.

It's over. Nice try, loser.

At least Rob's still here. I can't answer him for fear of being heard. But I'm not giving up, whatever he throws at me. No way.

I crawl round the far side and out again, straightening up and flattening myself against the side of the lorry. I'm between the second and third one now. I edge along towards the cab. There's a gap between the cab and the metal wagon behind, a flat metal neck with some thick coiled wires or pipes joining the two sections. I clamber up on to the metal platform. There's just enough room here, but no cover. I slither back down and duck under the back of the truck again. I've got a plan now. I'll stay underneath until they've loaded up and the driver's safely in the cab. Then I'll nip up to my perch on the neck.

It's drizzling outside, the air is damp and heavy. There are more feet in the yard now. My heart's starting to thud in my chest, but I know I can do it.

I warned you.

Mustn't let the pain distract me. I need to concentrate.

There's all sorts of shouting and joking about, and then the clattering of a metal shutter going up somewhere at the edge of the yard. The door of the cab of my lorry groans on its hinges as it's unlocked, yanked open and slammed shut again. The engine splutters into life. This is it. I've got to move, but there are people either side of the wagon. I can't get out now, I'll be right under their noses.

The noise of the engine is roaring in my ears and now some sort of warning noise is sounding, bleeping on and off and a recorded voice booming out. Either side of me, the wheels start to move, rolling slowly backwards. The bottom of the cab is coming towards me. Backwards? I've got no choice, I have to go too.

On my toes and knuckles I crawl like an ape across the yard, through pools of oil, sharp stones and puddles of water, keeping pace with the lorry's movement, I try to stay level with one set of wheels, so I can't be seen. The lorry creeps slowly across the yard and comes to a halt up against one of the buildings. The back doors are opened up and then a million feet are in and out above my head. I'm buzzing now. This lorry is definitely on its way today. If I keep my head, this is my ticket out of here. I'm gonna do it.

It takes about ten minutes and then the doors are slammed shut. This is it. I can't see any feet at my level. There are only the two other trucks across the yard and the bare concrete, dotted with puddles, their surfaces dancing now as the drizzle turns into rain.

The engine roars into life. It's got to be now. I scramble up to the front end, just behind the wheels, and then dart out round the wheel and up on to the neck. It's all over in a flash. I don't look round or to the side – I just focus on getting out and up, and now I'm here. I settle with my back to the cab, my feet braced against the trailer. I hold on to the pipes either side of me, well aware that there's nothing to stop me falling.

There's only one thing missing. Rob. The pain in my head has gone, but my clothes are still wet from last night and the rain's spotting down, even through the small gap between the cab and the wagon. So where is he?

The wagon's rolling forward now, and the butterflies in my stomach are more like bats, their wings knocking against the inside of my belly, their sharp little claws tearing it.

We're moving out of the yard now, easing between the buildings and heading for the drive.

Out of the corner of my eye, I see someone running past the lorry. So quick. A pale, white body, almost naked, running towards the front of the truck.

It's him.

The driver brakes and my head slams into the back of the cab. My ears are filled with the horn blaring a long continuous note, and the squealing protest as the discs grind against the wheel rims. The cab rocks, pushing my weight on to my legs and back again. The door's open now and the driver's feet thud on to the concrete as he jumps down from the cab. People are running from the yard behind us.

'Jesus! Jesus, help me!' The driver's shouting at the top of his voice, more of a scream than a bellow. A prayer screamed into the morning air.

'What's happened? What is it?' Voices from behind.

'I think I went over something.'

Men clatter past my hiding place. I freeze. There's nowhere to go, I've just got to sit tight.

'I can't look! Oh Jesus. I'm sorry, I'm sorry.'

'Calm down, Jimbo. Calm down.'

'I felt something, thought I saw something right at the last minute.'

'Saw what?'

'I dunno. A dog or a fox or ...'

'There's nothing under the cab. Stay there, mate, stay there, we'll look further down.'

I hold my breath and close my eyes. And I'm three years old, playing hide and seek. If I can't see, maybe I won't be seen. Raindrops land on my face, my hands.

Their sounds get nearer; feet scuffing on the ground, soft grunts as they bend down to look under.

Game's up, little brother. You lose.

So close now. I'm going to have to leg it. I open my eyes. To my left someone's back is level with me, horizontal as he peers under the wheels. Then a voice to my right: 'Oi! What the ...? Gotcha. It's a boy.' I swivel round. There's a bloke standing there, eyes nearly popping out of his head. He's a big bugger and he's reaching forward, about to collar me, so I go the other way. I jump on to my feet and step out on to the other fella's back, then leap off it on to the ground.

My stepping stone falls forward with a string of curses, and all the others are shouting at once.

'Here, stop him!'

'There he goes. Get him!'

There are half a dozen of them. I dodge the first couple. One of them grabs my coat, but I shrug it off and carry on running. Then someone tackles my legs and suddenly I'm down, face crunching into the concrete.

I'm surrounded by a circle of feet. Eventually someone hauls me upright. I look at the faces around me. There are six or seven men, all in overalls.

'What's your name, son? What are you doing here?'

'Are you English? You speak English?'

They're firing questions at me. Too many to answer. But I'm just waiting for a gap to appear in the crowd, for a chance to run away. One of the men looks at me long and hard. His face is almost as pale as Rob's, his lips bloodless.

'Was it you? Were you mucking about, running in front of my wagon?'

I don't answer.

'Here.' Someone holds my coat out towards me. 'Put this back on.'

'Thanks,' I say and the men around me visibly relax.

'You're English then, son. You from round here?'

Jimbo hasn't moved a muscle. He's still staring.

'Wait a minute, I know you. You're the one in the paper. The one whose brother ...'

He doesn't need to finish his sentence – they all know. An uneasy silence settles on the group.

No one's holding on to me any more.

I make a break for it, pushing through between Jimbo and his neighbour. I catch his shoulder as I go past, and there's no resistance. The impact turns him where he stands, a limp puppet whose strings have been cut, but his mates are quicker. Strong hands hold me back and I know I'm not going anywhere.

'Don't worry, son,' one of them says. 'You don't need to run. You're not in trouble. We'll see you get home now, safe and sound.'

Behind him, unseen by anyone else now, there's a shadow, a pale shape watching the drama play out. He puts one hand to his face, and then draws a figure 1 in the air.

Another victory.

One-nil to Rob.

TWENTY-TWO

Me and Neisha are sitting next to each other on the kiddies' swings at the play park on the rec, both moving gently backwards and forwards, trailing our feet on the soft ground beneath us.

'I thought … I thought you might've … you know.'

'What?'

'You know.'

Neisha doesn't want to meet my eye.

'Topped myself?' I say.

A quick flick up and then down again.

'Yeah. Your mum read me your note over the phone at half past five this morning. She was going out of her mind.'

'I only meant to tell her not to look for me.'

'She thought it meant "don't look, 'cause I don't want you finding the body."'

'Shit.'

'Yeah.'

Neisha rang soon after they brought me back. She wanted to see me, wouldn't take no for an answer. Meanwhile I put up with a tongue-lashing from Mum and Auntie Debbie and then tears and then another telling-off. The tears were threatening to spill out again when Neisha turned up, and suddenly I was caught between the sheer, pure joy of seeing her again and the massive sense of failure that I hadn't managed to get away, to take Rob away from her. There's something else, too. The burden of guilt – the sick weight of knowing that I goaded Rob into trying to kill her. It was all my fault.

Mum only agreed I could go out with her if I stayed within sight of home. It's not raining any more, but every hollow and dip in the path and playing field is full of lying water, and there's a sharp breeze ruffling the surface.

Bundled up in her anorak, hood up, Neisha looks at me through her thick brown lashes and it makes me want to stop all this, to tear up the script in my head where I talk to her about visions and voices and tell her what a bad person I am. I want to tell her that running away was a big mistake and I want to be with her, hold her, kiss her. But there's so much that she doesn't know ...

'So what *were* you doing?'

'Just running away.'

'And you weren't even going to say goodbye?'

She's hurt. I'm an idiot. Why didn't I think how hurt she would be?

'I was going to ring you. It just seemed for the best.

That you'd be better off without me.'

'How can you say that? I thought we … I thought you liked me.'

'I did. I do.'

'So what the fuck, Carl? I mean, what the fuck?'

I put my hand on her arm and she shrugs me off with a violence that takes me by surprise.

'I do, Neisha. Very much.'

'But?'

'What do you mean?'

'There's a "but" there. I "like you very much, but …"'

'I can't tell you. I'm not who you think I am. It's better if we don't, if we … if we … stop.'

It tears me apart to say it, but the effect on her is electric.

'Stop? So that's it, is it? Don't you want to shag me first, like your brother?'

She's stopped moving, grounded by her toes digging in to the asphalt. Her fingers are gripping the chain so hard that the skin is stretched shiny over her knuckles.

'Neisha, I—'

''Cause you're just the same, aren't you? You're not really interested in me. You don't really give a fuck.'

This is it. I can do it now, if I really want to. I can get her out of my life. I should. I must. To keep her safe.

'You're right, Neisha. We *are* the same. Me and Rob. That's why you should walk away. Because I'm no good for you. I never will be.'

But the words I thought would push her away have the opposite effect.

'You see,' she says, 'you see how wrong you are? You

saying that means that you *aren't* like him. You think you are but you aren't.'

Her shoulders relax a little and there's half a smile there.

'You silly, sweet thing. I know you. I know you better than you know yourself. You don't need to run away.'

I know I shouldn't, but I slip off the swing and stand in front of her. As I do so, the sun comes out, making all the wet surfaces around us sparkle. I can feel its warmth on the back of my neck. Neisha pulls me towards her. I stumble closer and she swings towards me, and now she's wrapping her legs round me.

'Steady,' I say, but, too late, the swing shifts from underneath her and she grabs me with her arms and instinctively I hold her tight. She's gripping me like a little monkey, and we're about to topple over. Without thinking, I try to bounce her higher and get my hands under her bum. But I can't get my balance and we're going to go over.

'Put your feet down. You'll have to put them down,' I yell. And she laughs and holds on even tighter.

'Neisha, put your feet down. I can't hold you!'

Finally she unwinds and plonks her feet on the ground.

'You're mental,' she says, checking me nervously to see if she's caused offence, 'in a good way,' she adds. 'In a good, good way.'

She puts her head back and laughs. My eyes follow the line of her throat down into the dark V of her anorak. And she moves her hand to the back of my neck and she tilts her head just the right amount so our lips meet as if it was the most natural thing in the world.

'Oh Neisha,' I breathe.

How can I keep away from this? From her?

'You won't leave me, will you?'

Her vanilla words transfer themselves from her tongue to mine.

'No, no, 'course not. I'll never leave you.'

We kiss for hours or minutes or seconds. Who knows how long? Some kids walk by and jeer at us, making lip-smacking, wellies-stuck-in-the-mud noises, but we keep our eyes closed and kiss and kiss until they've gone and we're alone again.

At some point, we draw apart. Neisha's face is blurry, like I've smudged her features with my mouth. We keep our arms round each other. I feel safe within this tight circle of her love. Safe and calm. The sun warms my neck and the world around us is silver and bright. The air carries the smell of chocolate from the factory and it mixes in my nostrils with Neisha's familiar sweetness. Even though part of me knows that it's wrong to be happy, I can't stop myself. This is how I am right now and it feels good – so, so good.

Neisha leans her head on my shoulder.

'You know you said you see him … Rob …' she says, and his name, hearing it spoken out loud, sends a dagger of ice between my ribs.

'Yeah?'

'Is he here now?'

Something about the way she asks makes me wonder

whether she wants him to be here – to see this, us. I move so I can see her face.

'No, not now,' I say.

Her hand at my waist relaxes just a tiny bit. A little bit of tension that I didn't even know was there has gone, and she blinks and smiles and kisses me, right next to my mouth.

'Good,' she says. 'Maybe he's gone.'

She disentangles one hand and lifts it up to stroke my hair. And I can't help thinking, There, there, the nasty boy's gone. And the voice in my head is his.

I shake my head violently and she holds her hand away, floating in mid-air.

'What?' she says.

'He's not gone, Neisha,' I say. 'He won't go until … unless …'

'Unless what?'

'Nothing.'

'Why do you think "he's" here? What's going to make "him" go?'

Her tone of voice. The tilt of her head. She doesn't believe me. She still thinks it's all in my mind.

I put my hands on the top of her arms, squeezing, maybe squeezing too tight.

'I'm not making this up.'

She shifts in my grip, but I don't let go.

'So how come you can see him and I can't?' She turns her head one way and then the other, looking behind her, all around.

'He's not here now, Neisha. And I don't know why I

can see him. I just can. I see him when I'm wet, that's all. The thing is … he's so angry now, I think something's changed. Somehow he's getting stronger.'

'Getting stronger?'

'Before, he was just a voice, a shape in the rain, but now he seems to be able to use the water against me, the weather even. The only thing that's the same is that when I'm dry he disappears.'

'What does he look like? Just the same as …?'

'He's how he was when they … when they fished him out of the water.'

She gasps.

'So why's he here?'

I let go of her and turn away.

'Don't ask me,' I say.

'Carl, you've got to tell me.'

'I can't.'

'Because of me, something to do with me?'

If I open my mouth now, I'm going get myself into trouble. I keep quiet, but it's just as bad.

'It is, isn't it?'

'No, 'course not,' I mumble.

I've still got my back to her. She darts round and ducks under so she's peering up into my face.

'Don't bullshit me, Carl. Don't ever bullshit me. You're rubbish at lying. What does he want?'

I twist away from her and start walking. She catches up and matches me, pace for pace.

'I'm not letting this go, Carl. You say you're being haunted. You want me to believe you, and I do, at least I'm trying to. But you have to be straight with me. What does he want, Carl? What does Rob want?'

I stop walking and face her. 'He wants to hurt you.'

'Hurt me?'

'Yeah. No. More than that. He wants to kill you, Neisha. And he wants me to help him. To prove my loyalty. To make me pay for killing him and for kissing you, fancying you … loving you …'

She's quiet for a moment. I'm not even sure if she heard me properly. Then her eyes soften.

'Loving me?'

'I'm sorry, it's too soon. Too much.'

'No. No …'

She reaches out to me and we draw together, holding each other close.

'But why does he hate me so much? Why can't he let it go? I don't understand what I did to deserve this.'

This is the moment, the chance to tell her the whole truth, get it out. I bottle it.

'You know he thought we were seeing each other, and then you threatened to tell about the burglary. It's just unfinished business in his eyes. That's why I pulled you away from the lake that time. That's why I made you promise not to go there. He wants you back there … he wants to drown you. So I want you to promise me again. Promise me that you'll never, never go back to the lake.'

I kiss the top of her head.

'Of course.'

'No, say it. Say it, Neisha. I need to hear it.'

'Carl, I promise you that I won't go back to the lake.'

'And you mean it?'

'Yes. Of course I do.'

'Because that's what all this is about, Neisha. That's why I ran away. I want to keep you safe. I love you, Neisha. I really love you.'

My words disappear into her mouth as she moves in and kisses me. She breathes them in, swallows them. And for a moment I'm lost again, in the sweet wet world we make together when we do this. And the warm swell of happiness is there again, and I catch myself thinking, 'It's going to be all right. I love her. She loves me. We're going to be okay.'

But even as I think this, I know it's not true. Because although everything I've said to her is the truth and I mean every word, I haven't told her the whole truth.

She thinks she's kissing Carl, the boy who saved her. She's not. She's kissing the boy who betrayed her.

TWENTY-THREE

When I kiss Neisha, really kiss her, it feels like the rest of the world is falling away. Or else it's shrinking down to this, to us, to the only thing that matters. It's shocking, delicious.

My senses concentrate on the soft place where we meet and this contact, a few square centimetres of flesh moving on flesh, sends messages out to every other cell in my body. I'm going to explode, or melt, or both. I'm naked, electric.

Even if I was wearing ten layers of clothes, I'd still be naked. And so would she. My naked body is connected to her naked body. And there's nowhere to hide.

And that's when I know I've got to say it. This naked moment. Because I've never felt like this before, and I want it to be perfect. I don't want to have any secrets. I want her to know me, to accept me, to love me.

I pull back from her and hold her a little away from me, so I can see her face.

'I need to tell you something,' I say. 'Something big. I should have told you as soon as I remembered it. I tried to tell you, I did try, but I couldn't get the words out.'

'What is it?'

It feels like the whole world has gone quiet. Like everyone and everything is waiting for what I'm going to say next.

'It was my fault.'

She shakes her head, tries to move forward, kiss me again, but I hold her back. Now there's tension between us, her pushing, me resisting.

'Carl, we've been through this. You did what you did to save me. Blaming yourself like this, it doesn't help.'

'No, not that.'

'What, then?'

I can feel her arms relaxing in my hands. She's ready to listen.

'It was my fault you were at the lake in the first place.'

''Course it wasn't. He wanted to see me, threatened me to make me go.'

I wish it was that simple. I wish I didn't have to say this.

'No. It was my fault. I said something to him that started this whole thing off. I'm to blame for all of this, because I was a coward, because he was taunting me about fancying you. I told him I didn't care about you at all, that I wouldn't even care if he killed you.'

'What?'

195

She's frozen now, like someone's pressed Pause and she's stopped, dead. I can't look at her any more.

'One time you got back together I heard you talking with him and you were laughing about me, you were telling him you didn't fancy me, would never fancy me. I was so … so crushed, Neisha, so jealous. It was a stupid thing to say. He thought I was daring him to do it. I was upset and in the heat of the moment … I said such a stupid, stupid thing.'

I thought it was quiet before, but this is something else.

I squint at her through half-shut eyes. This is bad, really bad. Her face is sagging with shock, jaw slack. But it's her eyes that get me. They're pooling with tears.

'I don't understand. I thought you liked me. You just said you loved me,' she says.

'I did. I do. I love you, Neisha, I always have.'

'So how could you …?'

'I wanted Rob to stop hitting me, and I was angry because you didn't want me. It was only for a moment, and then I'd said it and I thought Rob would forget it. But he didn't.'

I can't talk any more. I just stand and wait for her to start on me. But she doesn't. She shrugs me off and turns away, starts walking out of the play park. Her hands are rammed in her pockets, her shoulders are up and her face is down.

I watch for a second or two, then go after her.

'Neisha,' I call out.

She doesn't turn round.

I vault over the fence and land in front of her. She tries

to walk past, turning her head away. I step into her path. She dodges the other way and I grab her arm.

'Don't!' she spits out. 'Don't touch me.'

I keep hold of her, and under her clothes her arm muscles are taut.

'I just wanted you to know the truth.'

'And now I do.'

Our eyes meet for a moment and it feels like my eyeballs are vaporising in the heat of her hatred.

Everything's changed.

I've lost her.

'That was the old me, though,' I say quickly. I'm not like that any more. I'm—'

'Shut up, Carl. Just shut the fuck up.'

'But—'

'I don't want to hear it. Any of it.'

She shakes my hand off her arm and breaks away.

'Neisha—'

She turns to face me.

'I thought you were different, Carl, but you were the same as him. You *are* the same. I hate you. I fucking hate you, Carl.'

And then she's away. And I'm standing next to the kids' play park, watching her run out of my life. How can this be happening when I still have the taste of her in my mouth?

The sun's gone in. Everything that was silver before is dull grey and green and brown. I shiver and look up and there's a massive cloud blotting out half the sky, moving rapidly from left to right.

I'm in the lake with a half-and-half sky above me, thrashing through the water. I can't see them any more. Neisha and Rob. The first flash of lightning scares the crap out of me, but it reveals them in its strobe light. Two heads above the water.

My legs are like jelly. I've got to get out of this. I've got to get home. Neisha's disappeared from view and I turn and start running for home. The first raindrop hits the top of my ear, and his voice bursts into my head, clear and close. And then the sky opens and it's as if someone is tipping water from a bucket on to the rec and the street and the flats. People outside the shop scream as they're soaked in an instant. The cold, the shock of it, takes my breath away.

I'm coming for you Cee. You can't stop me.

I try to wipe the water out of my eyes and keep running. Around me, people are scattering in panic. Rob stands in the middle of the rec, not pursuing me, just standing, his pale figure the only still thing in a world alive with water.

Kill her or I'll kill you.

'Get away from me! Leave me alone!'

The concrete steps up to the flats are awash, turned into a waterfall. I fight my way up and stagger along the walkway, blast through the front door and slam it shut behind me.

You can't shut me out.

He's still here. Close.

I climb up the stairs and go into my room. Our room. The curtains are closed. The smell in the air sticks to my skin. It invades my lungs and makes them tighten, closing down, trying to shut out the spores. I can't see anything in the gloom. I flick on the light and I wish I hadn't. The wall by my mattress is black now. Black and stinking and oozing. Beads of liquid sit wetly on the surface. In the corner above Rob's bed, the place where the stain started, water is trickling down the wall. It's coming in. It's coming for me.

I can't stay here. I can't.

I'll just change my clothes and get out. I strip off then bend forward and start rummaging through the heaps. Everything is clammy to the touch. I burrow into another pile, flinging them behind me and out of the door as I sort through. I can't find anything.

Everything's musty, damp, nasty. I don't want it next to my skin.

'Carl, what's the problem?'

I look over my shoulder. Mum's in the doorway. She catches the last thing I threw, a football shirt.

'There's nothing to wear. Everything's wet,' I say.

She looks at the shirt in her hand.

'Everything stinks. I can't get away from it. I just want to get dry, Mum. I can't get dry ...'

She's looking at me now, almost like she's frightened of me, and then her gaze shifts to the wall beyond.

'Jesus Christ,' she says. 'That wall's running with damp. How long has it been like this?'

'What?'

I'm trying to block out Rob's voice, focus on Mum, work out what she's saying.

'How long has—? Oh never mind, just get some clothes on, can't you?'

Listen to Mum. Get some clothes on. Get dressed. But everything's damp.

She fucking hates you now, Cee ...

'I can't, Mum. I can't wear these. I can't, I can't, I can't, I can't ...'

I push past her on to the landing. I'm stark naked, but I don't care. Debbie's halfway up the stairs. She gives a little shriek when she sees me and retreats back into the lounge.

'Oh my Gawd, Kerry. He's gone mad again! Shall I call the police?'

'No, don't call anyone!' Mum shouts back. Then to me, 'Cover yourself up, Carl, for God's sake.' She thrusts the football shirt at me.

'No, it's no good, Mum. I can't wear it!' I throw it down the stairs.

She turns to me.

'This has got silly now. Calm down.' But Mum's anything but calm. Her face is red and the veins on her neck are bulging. 'Calm down!!' she bellows, but I'm spinning round in the hallway now, not knowing where to go, what to do, just whirling round, trying to make it all go away.

'Wait there. Just wait,' she screams. She's gone, but only for a minute. She comes back and catches my arm. I keep turning and my arm twists behind my back until I'm brought to a halt. I unwind so that I'm facing her.

'Here,' she says. 'Put this on.'

She's holding a dressing gown. Her dressing gown. Baby pink and a bit ratty. She helps me thread my arms through the holes and wraps it round me, doing the cord up with a knot.

I stretch the top of it up and hold it to my face. It's soft and smells of cigarette smoke and deodorant and perfume. I breathe in and out a few times and my own breath mixes with the dressing gown smells and it feels like my face is in a tent or a mask or something, a close little world that's different from outside.

My breathing slows down. I realise I can't hear Rob any more. It's quiet. The whole house is quiet.

'Is that better?' Mum says.

I can't speak. Not yet.

'Sit down a minute,' she says, and I obey. She crouches next to me.

She reaches into her pocket and pulls out a packet of fags and her lighter. Her hands are shaking as she lights up and inhales. 'That's it,' she says. 'We're fine now, aren't we? Do you want a drag?'

I shake my head. She tips her head back as she exhales.

'You got yourself in a bit of a state, didn't you?' she says. 'But I can see why. I didn't know your room was that bad. That's not right, that isn't. I'll ring the housing people. We'll get it sorted. And I'll take your clothes down the launderette, get them cleaned up, shall I? You can't live like this. No one can live like this.'

She takes another drag.

'I've let things get a bit out of hand, Carl. I'm sorry.'

'No, Mum. You don't understand. It's not this place. I think I'm going mad.'

She slumps down to the floor. I've still got my hand on

her arm and now she puts both of her hands on mine so we're holding each other ... at arm's length.

"Course you're not. You just had a bad day, that's all.'

'I want to go somewhere, Mum. Get some help.'

Take me back to the hospital room, I want to say, the place they took me after the lake – warm and clean and bright.

'I'm here, Carl. I'm right here for you. I'll help you.'

'But I hear him, Mum. He talks to me. I see him too.'

'You and me both, Carl. I see him everywhere.'

'No, you don't understand ...'

She sighs. 'I see him in the bath, when he was a tot. Could never get him to go in and then when he did couldn't get him to come out. Bloody terror. I see him in the kitchen eating stuff straight out of the tin. I see him on the sofa, next to me, watching those films, pretending he's not scared. He's still here, Carl, isn't he? He always will be.'

My heart sinks. It's not the same.

'You remember him, that's all,' I say.

'Yeah,' she says, 'like you do. It's normal. It's okay. You're okay. Come here.'

She pulls me towards her and puts her arms round me. I let myself be drawn in, not hugging her back, but not resisting.

'It's going to be all right,' she says. 'It's going to be all right.'

I close my eyes, and I see his face, his eyes wide open, and the zip passing up and over, sealing him in. I try to sit up, but Mum's holding tight.

'I've gotta go, Mum. I can't stay here.'

I can't break away from her, and now I can feel her body shaking.

'Don't leave me,' she says. 'Please, Carl, don't leave me. We'll be all right. I promise we will.'

She's crying, sobbing into my neck.

There's a knock at the door.

Below us, Debs opens the door and starts talking to someone. Odd words and phrases drift up the stairs.

'Hit her … stark naked … completely wild … brother at the lake … safety …' Debs must have called the police after all.

Mum's rocking us both now, side to side.

'You're all I've got left. Don't leave me. Don't leave me, Carl.'

'Miss Adams?'

Someone's calling up. Mum stops rocking.

'Miss Adams?'

She takes a deep breath. 'Just a minute,' she shouts down.

She gives me one last squeeze then lets go. She wipes her face on her sleeve and takes a couple more breaths.

'You don't want to leave really, do you?'

Yes, yes, a million times yes.

'I dunno. I can't sleep in there, Mum. I just can't do it.'

'How about the sofa?'

I shrug.

'Just hang on until the funeral. We'll get through this together. We will, Carl. I promise. Okay?'

She makes her way downstairs. I bring my knees up inside my pink skirt and rest my head on them, listening as she tries to do an impression of someone normal. Asking the cops to come in, saying 'Isn't the rain shocking?' and 'Can I get you some tea?'

The front door closes again and the voices get quieter, more muffled, as they all move into the lounge. Suddenly exhausted, I tune out, letting their conversation become noise, not words, a background murmur that's strangely soothing.

After ten minutes or so, Mum comes upstairs. She kneels next to me.

'They want to talk to you, check that you're okay. You should get dressed.'

'I'm all right like this.'

The dressing gown's like a comforting blanket. I'm dry and warm now. I don't mind if I never take it off.

'I don't think so.' She glances at the jumble sale of clothing trailing along the landing and then goes into her room. She reappears with some jeans and a T-shirt.

'Whose—?'

'Don't ask,' she says. 'I couldn't find any pants.'

I take the clothes from her. I stand up and turn my back as I step into the jeans and pull them up. They're a couple of sizes too big and I can't help thinking about mum's weird record when it comes to boyfriends and shuddering. I slip the dressing gown off and dive into the T-shirt. I look down at the illustration on the front, turning my head sideways to make out the writing: 'Surfers do it standing up.'

I look back at Mum.

She pulls a face. 'Sorry,' she says and I know she's not

just apologising for this shitty shirt. In spite of everything I find myself smiling, feel a laugh tickling at the back of my throat.

'Jesus, Mum,' I say.

'I know.'

I bend forward and turn the bottom of the legs up, folding each hem twice until they skim the top of my feet.

'You okay now? You ready?' she asks.

'Yeah. Okay.'

Later, when they've all gone and Debbie's taken herself off 'for a soak' in the bath, Mum makes a bed for me on the sofa. She's slept there often enough, or rather fallen unconscious and stayed there, but this is different. She takes the back cushions off and fetches a pillow and my sleeping bag. When I see it, I get a choking feeling. Even across the room I can smell the mustiness. The zip catches the light and I hear the noise of the other zip, the one that sealed him in, and the panic rises up in me, along with the contents of my stomach.

'I can't, Mum,' I say. 'Not the sleeping bag.'

She purses her lips, but she doesn't say anything. She takes it upstairs and comes back again with a sheet and a couple of blankets.

'Better?'

'Yeah.'

'I should get you a duvet,' Mum says. 'They had them in the supermarket a couple of weeks ago. Only a fiver. But it was a fiver I didn't have. Well, I would've needed a tenner, because there were two of you ...' She lapses into silence. Then, 'God, Carl, how are we going to do this?'

I deliberately choose to misunderstand her; I don't want to talk about big stuff, not now.

'Just spread the sheet out on the sofa and I'll have the blankets on top.'

She looks confused for a moment.

'Yeah … right. Okay.'

She shakes out the sheet and starts tucking it in.

'We're going to see him tomorrow,' she says.

'What?'

'Me and Debbie. We're going to view his … visit the … we're going to say goodbye to him at the Chapel of Rest.'

I pretend to be doing something to the pillow.

'You should come. It's the right thing to do, Carl. We've always done it in my family. It helps.'

The hairs are standing up on the back of my neck at the thought of seeing him again, seeing his body how I last saw it.

She's laid the blankets on top of the sheet, tucked them in at the back and the sides. I put the pillow at one end and it looks like a proper bed.

'Will you be all right here?'

'Yeah, I reckon.' To be honest, it looks a lot nicer than where I usually sleep.

'I'll go up, then,' she says. 'I'm done in. I bet Debs will crash too after her bath. She won't bother you.'

'Does she have to stay here?' I ask, feeling guilty as I say it.

'It's only a couple of days. I know she's a pain, but she's trying to help. She'll go after the funeral.'

'Then it'll just be you and me here.'

'Here … or somewhere.'

'What?'

'I rang the housing people. They said they know about the damp. It's not just us. The rain's been so bad lately. They don't seem to know what to do. It's the whole block. The roof needs doing, all sorts of stuff. They might even move us.'

The rain's pelting down, battering against the window, with no let-up.

'Would you mind if we went somewhere else?'

'I dunno. No, I don't think so.'

'Don't want to stay for the memories?'

Memories. God, too many memories.

She doesn't wait for an answer, but starts heading for the stairs.

'Mum,' I call after her. She pauses. 'I'm a bit cold. Can I have your dressing gown, just for tonight?'

She starts to say something and then she stops herself. 'Yes,' she says, with the trace of a smile. 'I'll bring it down.'

Later, with the soft cotton next to my skin and the blankets drawn up under my chin, I listen to the wind and rain battering against the window. They can't reach me here and neither can Rob. Tonight, I'm safe.

I think of Neisha and I wonder if she's lying in bed listening too. What happened between us today doesn't seem real. To get so close, to feel her warmth healing me, making everything seem better, and then to break apart so violently. To hear her shouting that she hates me. My stomach flips when I remember her voice, the look in her eyes. But there's a hint of another feeling too. A small sensation that I've won something.

I couldn't bear to push her away, but it happened anyway, and it's the best thing I could have done. Because she'll stay away from me now. She'll stay away from me and Rob. And he won't be able to hurt her. It's shitty but it's true. The more she hates me, the safer she'll be.

It doesn't matter if I grow old and lonely without her. It doesn't matter if I never have sex. It doesn't matter if the voices in my head drive me over the edge. If I can keep Neisha safe, it will all be worth it.

And now, tucked up on my makeshift bed, with thoughts of Neisha in my head, I've got some of that warmth back. It's not the same as holding her, kissing her, but it will have to do.

The sound of water on glass starts lulling me off to sleep. The room's softly dark but as I close my eyes, it seems like the top corner where the wall meets the ceiling is darker than the rest, that there's a patch that wasn't there when Mum turned the light off. I tell myself I'm imagining it. I'm warm and dry and sleepy.

I close my eyes and pull my blankets up a bit further.

Night, Cee.

My eyes are open again. In a flash, I'm bathed in a cold sweat.

It's going to be another long night.

TWENTY-FOUR

The rain doesn't let up all night. And neither does Rob. Every time I get to the edge of sleep, he's there. A word in my ear. The sound of his breath.

You're running out of time, little brother.

At one point the blankets start slipping off and I jerk into consciousness. Was it him? Did he move them? And all the time, I'm thinking about the dark patch in the corner — thinking of it creeping towards me, stinking silently.

You're running out of time, cowardly bastard.

His voice is like a tap dripping. A noise repeated over and over again. He's only whispering, but my mind turns it into something bigger, until each word is a hammer blow, and when he's quiet I'm listening, cowering, anticipating the next strike. And beneath it all, mixed up in it, the kitchen tap is dripping – no, it's more than a drip, it's running now. And the pipe in the wall is gurgling – the tap in the bathroom upstairs must be running too.

Eventually I crawl into the kitchen and slump on to one of the chairs. I fold my arms on the table and rest my head on them. The rain's still hammering at the window, but that doesn't bother me too much. What gets me is the kitchen tap. And the more I try to tune it out the more my mind focuses on it.

I get up and go over to the sink. I wrench the tap round until it won't move any more, but the water keeps coming. Jesus Christ! It's only a tap. Surely I can turn the bloody thing off. I try again, almost expecting it to shear off in my hands.

I grab a tea-towel from the back of one of the chairs and put it in the sink. And the sound's almost gone, just a dull, damp suggestion of a noise.

Back at the kitchen table I get my head down again. I'm so tired, I don't think anything's going to stop me sleeping now. I can't hear his voice any more. I can't smell him. I pull the collar of the dressing gown further up and close my eyes.

But the water soon saturates the cloth. The sound that was muffled grows louder and louder. Water falling on wet cloth.

Time's up.

I sit up.

'For God's sake, Rob, leave me alone. You're dead. You're dead. I've seen you dead.'

My voice is the voice I've used during fifteen years of bickering and fighting, pleading and teasing. The voice I use when I talk to my brother. But the words are mad. They're not words I ever thought I'd say. If anyone else heard them, if there was anyone here except him and me, they'd be backing away quickly now or ringing the men in white coats.

'Who are you talking to?'

I swivel round.

Mum's in the doorway.

'No one. I dunno, Mum. Him. Rob. He's here. He's still here.'

'He's not here. Not like that,' she says. 'There's no one here but you and me.'

'But he is. It's the tap and the rain and the mould and everything. It's him. It's him, Mum.'

She doesn't back away or reach for her phone. She steps forward and strokes my hair.

'Shh,' she says. 'That's enough, now. It's not real, Carl. It's not real. You're coming with us tomorrow – well, later today now. It'll help. I promise.'

'What time is it now?'

'Half-four. You been asleep?'

'No.'

She strokes my hair again. 'Me neither. Shall I put the kettle on?'

'Whatever.'

'We could see what's on the telly.'

'I can't … I can't sit in there,' I say. 'The thing, the damp – it's coming down the wall.'

'Really?'

She flicks the lounge light on and curses.

'This place,' she says. 'You wouldn't house a pig here.' She turns the light off again and walks into the kitchen. 'Let's try the radio.'

There's some sort of mushy music on. Mum turns the volume right down, while she makes us both a cup of tea.

'What's this tea-cloth doing here?' She picks up one corner with her index finger and thumb.

'Nothing. I was trying to stop the tap dripping, stop the noise, that's all.'

She pulls a face and drapes the cloth on the edge of the sink. Then she has a go at tightening the tap, gives up, sets our mugs on the table and sits opposite me. Her face is crumpled and old. Her eyes are bloodshot from the booze and lack of sleep. But she's calm. A lot calmer than me.

The music fades and a tired-sounding DJ comes on.

'It's a rainy night in Georgia, and it's a rainy night right here, that's for sure. I've actually got a weather warning for you. The Met Office say that given the level of ground-water over the past few days, this new rain is likely to bring localised flooding. So stay safe, people. Stay inside and turn the radio up. Here's Travis ...'

'It's never going to stop fucking raining, is it? We're all going to drown at this rate,' Mum says, sipping her tea. Then she realises what she's said and looks up at me, stricken. 'God ... what am I saying? Carl, you know I didn't mean ...'

'It's okay,' I say, and find myself reaching across the

table and putting my hand on top of hers and giving it a little squeeze. 'It's okay. It's only words.'

We're all going to drown.

But underwater or not, I feel like I'm drowning now.

TWENTY-FIVE

The body lies on a bed in the middle of the room. The covers are over his bottom half, and he's wearing a sort of gown, like a nightie. It's so clean, cleaner and whiter than anything we've got at home, and so's he. I was expecting him, his corpse, to be how he comes to me now – streaked with mud, dripping wet, oozing water. But he's not like that at all. His skin is smooth and dry, with no marks on his face. His hair's been washed and dried. His eyes are closed. At first glance he looks as though he's asleep.

But this is just a body. An empty body.

It isn't Rob, not really. It's a shell, something that used to belong to him. Part of me is horrified, shocked at being in the same room as his … as this.

I force myself to look at the bed and then I look away.

Well, I've done it now. I've 'viewed the body' and I'm ready to leave, but Mum moves forward to stand next to his head and as she's clutching my hand, tightly, I have no choice but to go with her. Debbie stays just inside the door, silent for once, hand clasped to her mouth.

Outside the wind howls and sighs, throwing rain against the small, high stained-glass window above the head of the bed.

Mum's face is alive, twitching and wobbling, her emotions bubbling and writhing under her skin, waiting to burst out. And then they come, with a great heaving sigh and huge, wet, ugly sobs. She lets go of my hand and bends over him, resting her head on his chest. Her movements, her convulsions, shaking the body and the bed.

I look round, worried whether she's allowed to touch him, make all this noise. The woman in the black suit who showed us in is still here, standing near the door, next to Debbie. Her feet are planted solidly apart, hands clasped gently in front of her. She sees me looking and her mouth moves a little, not a smile, not quite, something else – something that says this is okay.

Debbie darts forward.

She puts her arm across Mum's back and leans down so her face is close to Mum's. They're both crying now. Their noise fills the small room. It's out of control, so out of control, it's almost frightening. I'm embarrassed for them, I desperately want them to stop, but then I suddenly think, it's not them who are embarrassing, it's me.

I killed him. I killed my brother. I took him away from

Mum. Yet I'm standing here like a plank of wood. I don't feel anything. What's wrong with me?

I'm aware of Suit-Woman's eyes on me and the urge to leave, to walk out of here, gets stronger. I shouldn't have come. I didn't want to. I turn to go, but somehow Mum notices.

'Carl!' she wails. 'Carl, come here!'

She opens her arms and I go to her. What else can I do? Both she and Debbie wrap me up so I'm nearly smothered. Their coats are wet from the rain. Their faces are wet from their tears. And now I'm wet too.

They hold me and rock me and cry. Close to, the sound is distorted, barely human. It's the sound of raw distress, and it starts to get to me. Everything still feels unreal, but I'm starting to believe it now, the whole sequence of events: the old lady, the necklace, Neisha and Rob, and the lake. It was all leading here, to this sad, stark room. To a body on a bed.

I peer over Mum's shoulder and he's here, over by the wall, watching.

Rob. The other Rob. Mud-streaked and dripping. His mouth is open, and brown liquid trickles out of both sides.

I close my eyes and open them again. He's closer this time. Now his lips are moving.

You owe me.

Even above Mum and Debbie's noise, I can hear him, loud and clear.

I can't wait for you any longer.

A big fat ball of something is growing inside me.

It swells and grows harder, pushing up against my diaphragm and my ribs, stopping me breathing.

Time's up, Cee.

I can see the pores in his face, leaking, oozing. I can see the foetid water leaking from his eye sockets.

It's still growing, the thing inside me, pressing down on my guts, squeezing my bowels. My legs are shaky. I don't know how this is going to end. It feels like whatever this is, it's too big to come out of me. It'll rip me to shreds.

Some part of me twitches and an odd retching noise comes out of my mouth. My throat is desperately sore and my eyes are stinging.

'That's right, Carl,' Mum says, 'let it out. It's okay.'

Someone's rubbing my back and convulsions start rippling through me. And I'm underwater again, with the pressure inside and the pressure outside building until it's unbearable.

I need air. I've got to get air.

I gulp and swallow but nothing will stay down now. Whatever's inside me is on its way out, and here it comes, bursting from my mouth and my nose and my eyes.

I buckle forward, but Mum and Debbie prop me up.

'It's okay. It's okay. Let it out.'

There's another noise now, coming from inside me, drowning everything else out – Mum, Debbie, Rob. A harsh, thick, grating sound. A strangled, tearing, cry of agony.

They can't hold me. I crash to the floor and now I'm on my hands and knees, tears pouring off my face, strings of

217

drool spooling out of my mouth. I can't stop it, whatever it is – grief, self-pity, anger, terror. It's taken me over in its tidal wave. I'm being swept along, powerless to do anything but go with it until it stops.

I see his feet in front of me, toes bent like claws, mud under the toenails. The sound, my noise, is reverberating round my head, but his voice breaks though again.

I'll get you and I'll get her. No one can stop me. I'll kill you all!

My mind gropes for the word. My tongue and lips try to find the right shape, to form themselves around this noise, mould it into something that makes sense. Something that will stop this, once and for all.

I close my eyes again and scream.

'No. NO! NOOO!'

'It's all right. It's all right.' Mum's crouching next to me. She puts her hands either side of my face, wiping the tears and spit with her thumbs. I open my eyes. All I can see is her, her face blotchy and wet.

My jaw presses down into her hand as I open my mouth and yell.

'NOOOO!'

Saliva gushes out and is caught between my skin and hers, but she doesn't flinch. She's here for me, even though her face is creased with concern.

'Carl. Carl. It's all right. I love you. It's gonna be all right.'

The room turns icy cold. There's a sharp bang, the sound of breaking glass and a woman screaming.

Mum and I look up. It's Suit-Woman screaming. Her hands are up by her face and she's staring at the wall above the bed. The metal framework of the stained glass window is still there, but most of the glass has gone. A few bits are left, like broken teeth clinging on in a mouth that's been punched out. And now rain comes in horizontally through the black gap. A few drops hit me, but most of them spatter the body on the bed.

I scramble to my feet.

Suit-Woman's trying to get herself together.

'I'll have to ask you to leave,' she says shakily, stepping towards us, indicating the way to the door.

'What's happening?' Mum asks. I help her up from the floor.

'The storm!' Debbie wails. 'It's blown the window in.'

No one else seems to notice that there's no glass inside the room. That something blew the window out.

'Please, I need to ask you to leave. I'm sorry.' Suit-Woman puts one hand on Mum's shoulder.

'I need to say goodbye,' Mum says. 'One minute. One minute, that's all.'

The white gown is blotched with raindrops now, turning the fabric see-through, making it cling to the cold flesh beneath. The skin on Rob's face is wet. The pillow and the covers are wet. Mum wipes him gently with a tissue, leans forward and kisses him.

'Carl, do you want to ... to say something?'

I look down at the body. There's a blast of air from outside, bringing little brown leaves mixed up in the rain. A couple settle on the body's face. Small, dark flecks of stuff, that look for a moment like mud.

'Oh my God, oh my God.' Mum wipes at his face again,

her actions panicky this time. As she dabs at him, his head moves under her fingers.

She gasps and a high, frightened squeal escapes from her lips.

'Leave him, Mum,' I say. 'It's time to go.'

'Miss Adams, I'm so sorry. I'm so sorry this happened. We'll clean him up, I promise. We'll look after him.'

'I can't leave him. Not like this ...'

'It's not him, Mum. Not really,' I say. 'He's gone, Mum. Rob's gone.'

And looking round the room, I really think he has. It's not just that I can't see him or hear him any more. It feels different. There's nothing left of Rob here any more.

Debbie and me steer Mum out into the waiting room. The wind from the broken window ruffles the plastic flowers in their vases. A few little bits of leaf have settled on the carpet.

Suit-Woman is almost back in control of herself. She smoothes down her skirt and says, 'I want to offer you a sincere apology. That's never happened before. It was unacceptable. I was very ... unprofessional. I'm so sorry.'

Mum looks at her, a bit bewildered.

'It wasn't your fault,' Debbie says. 'It's this weather, isn't it?' The wind's rattling the door to the outside now. 'S'pose we'll have to go out in it again.'

Suit-Woman looks around her.

'I can offer you an umbrella.'

'We've got some, ta,' says Debbie. 'Not that they're going to be much use, it's coming down so hard. We'll just have to brave it. Thank you, though. Thank you for everything.' She looks at Mum and me. 'Are we ready?'

I thought I was. I wanted to get out of here right at the beginning, but now I'm not so sure.

Rob's not in here, after all. So he must be out there. Somewhere in the storm.

TWENTY-SIX

Mum and Debbie walk towards the door, but I lag behind.

'Carl?' Mum says. She walks back to me, a little unsteady on her feet and links her arm through mine. 'You hold me up and I'll hold you up,' she says. 'Okay?'

I pull the hood of my sweatshirt up, and the hood of my jacket on top of that, yanking them as far forward as possible, then ease my sleeves down over my fingers and put them in my pockets. I know they're giving me funny looks, but no one says anything.

'Okay,' I say, and Debbie opens the door.

None of us are ready for the force of the air that hits us. It whistles through the room, buffeting us where we stand. Papers blow off the reception desk and into the chapel behind us.

'Oh, good Lord!' Suit-Woman sets off after them. We leave her to it and push our way outside.

It's two in the afternoon, but it's so dark it feels like the middle of the night. There's water everywhere now, the streets are running with it. The few people we see are splashing along, leaning into the wind, or being blown forwards, legs scrambling to keep up with their bodies.

I keep my head down. Debbie's the other side of Mum, arm in arm, and together we battle our way out of the high street and turn the corner by the old people's bungalows, half-walking, half-running. We pass a line of people, heaving bags of sand to each other, piling them up outside the front doors. I look up and Harry's standing by his window. He raises his hand and I nod in return.

Another time when I ran away from here in the dark comes into my mind.

We leave the back door open and run. The woman is lying on the floor. I catch up with Rob.

'Shall we ring someone? Dial 999?'

'Shut up and keep running.'

'But she's in trouble ... she's ...'

'I said shut up. So do it. Shut it.'

Now Harry's on his own. And Rob ... Rob's out here somewhere.

Rain is already getting in through the tunnel of my double hood and seeping through the seams of my coat. My trainers are wet through and so are Mum's and Debbie's. The water on the road seems to be getting deeper by the minute. I keep looking round, expecting to see him, hear him. He must appear soon, it's just a question of when and where.

We walk up the alleyway, heading for the rec. It's too narrow to walk together, so we form a line, with me bringing up the rear. Maybe it will be here – in this dark, confined space. He'll stand in my path and I won't know whether to stop or try and walk past him, through him.

No sooner have I thought that than we're out in the open again and he still hasn't appeared. The wind is whipping the stunted trees by the side of the path. Mum and Debbie cling on to each other again, but I don't join them. I stop and look around. The rain's sheeting down. I pull my right hand out of my pocket and hold it out, palm upwards. It's wet in an instant. Water starts to pool in the middle of the palm, trickling down my fingers and splashing in from the heavens.

The only sound is the sound of the storm, wet footsteps, the wind in the trees. His voice isn't here.

I open my eyes. Mum and Debbie are twenty metres ahead, huddled together. There's no one else on the rec. Over by the shops, someone runs from the doorway of Ashraf's shop to their car, holding a plastic bag over their head.

I scan the corners of the field, the gateways for a pale figure. I can't see him anywhere. I pull both my hoods down and tip my head back, tilting my face to the sky, trying and failing to keep my eyes open as the raindrops hurtle towards them. I blink the water out of them and look again.

He's not here.

I've spent days being terrified, dreading the dripping of a tap, the hint of dampness in the air. And now this. Water drips off my hair and trickles down my neck.

No Rob.

I unzip my coat and take it off, pull my jumper and T-shirt over my head. The rain's shockingly cold but I don't care. It stings as it hits my skin. I drop my clothes on the ground and hold my arms out horizontally, palms up, face up, mouth open.

A gust of wind buffets me nearly off the path, and I find I'm laughing.

He's gone. He's really gone.

I don't need to be scared any more.

I'm not going mad.

And then it hits me. He's gone. He's really gone. My brother's dead. I killed him.

My arms drop by my sides. The rain keeps hammering down and it's not exhilarating any more and I'm cold. Cold and soaked and stupid and alone.

All that's left of my brother is the body we just saw. The rest has gone, and that will be gone, too, tomorrow.

Rob's gone. I killed him.

Water drips off the end of my nose and my chin. I stand like a statue and let it drip.

'Carl? Carl, what are you doing?' Mum and Debbie are running towards me. 'Carl, what's happened?'

Mum slows up and bends down to pick up the clothes I dropped.

'Carl! Carl! You're soaked. Don't just stand there. Come on, let's get home. Come on.'

They're both fussing round me like a couple of crows pecking at roadkill. And that's what I feel like. Something dead and empty. Something useless and rotting. Something squashed flat by a passing lorry.

They're pushing and pulling at me now, and I let myself be dragged across the rec, along the parade and up the steps at the back. I'm very, very cold and very, very tired.

'I'll run you a bath. Don't argue. A nice hot bath will do you the world of good,' Debbie says, clattering up the stairs.

I glance into the lounge. The black stain is floor to ceiling now on one side of the room. A thick dark stripe. The familiar twang of decay is there, but Rob is not.

'Get yourself upstairs and into that tub,' Mum says.

I don't move.

'You don't want me to take you up there and bath you, do you?' The threat breaks through my numbness.

'No, no, I'm all right. I'm going.'

I squeeze past Debbie on the landing. She won't look me in the eye. I suppose she's nervous being this close to a nutter, or maybe it's the whole shirtless thing. Whatever, she can't get by me and down the stairs quick enough.

I close the bathroom door and slide the bolt to. Water thunders into the bath, sending up a cloud of steam. At the sink the tap is dribbling. A lifetime ago, when I'd just got back from hospital, this was the first thing that really freaked me out. I reach out now and turn it clockwise. And it stops.

The bath water is nearly up to the rim. I peel off my wet socks, jeans and pants and turn off both taps. I'm about to step in when I get a flash of a picture in my head, an image of Rob, his pale body lying on the bottom of the bath. It's not the Rob who's been haunting me. It's the one I just saw lying on a bed in a clean white gown. His eyes are closed. His face is clean.

It's not him, I tell myself. It's not him.

And it isn't. It's just my brain processing everything, trying to deal with it all. I wonder if there will ever be a time when water will just be water to me. I wonder if I'll ever forget what he looks like.

I look at the bath again. There's no one here. It's just a tub full of clean, steaming water. I step in and lower myself down, every inch of me zinging as my frozen skin meets the heat. For a minute I think I've misjudged it and I'm going to be scalded, but as my body temperature adjusts, I relax a little. The water's hot, but not too hot. It's just right, delicious even.

I lie with my knees bent and my head propped against one end, breathing in the steamy air. It's the first bath I've had in nearly a week. The first time I've been able to really relax …

I try to clear my mind and just focus on being here. Now.

Today was weird and frightening. Tomorrow's going to be difficult. Breathe slowly. Let everything go. Just for a few minutes. Let it all go and enjoy the warmth.

But I can't do it. Something's niggling away in my head and some words from Harry's book are there. The end of the story.

And George raised the gun and steadied it, and he brought the muzzle of it close to the back of Lennie's head. The hand shook violently, but his face set and his hand steadied. He pulled the trigger. The crash of the shot rolled up the hills and rolled down again. Lennie jarred, and then settled slowly forward to the sand, and he lay without quivering.

It ends in death. And I've got a terrible feeling that this story hasn't reached the end yet. Rob hasn't got a gun. It won't happen with a bullet in the back of a head. But he's not finished. I know the ending. If I think hard, look inside myself, the answer's there.

I start to panic again. I'm wet. As wet as I can be without dunking my head under. So where is he? At the chapel, he threatened to kill us all. And that window didn't shatter on its own. Something punched it out. And then he went ... where? He hasn't come home with me. I don't believe he's actually, finally gone, to heaven or hell or wherever's next.

I rack my brains to remember what he said.

I'll get you and I'll get her. No one can stop me. I'll kill you all!

Does that mean he doesn't need my help any more, that he can kill by himself?

And then I remember the power of his anger, the way he seems to control the water around him. He's not here, so he must be somewhere else. With someone else.

Time's up.

Neisha. She's not safe. She's not safe at all.

TWENTY-SEVEN

I leap out of the bath, water dripping off me. I don't bother to towel myself – I just duck out of the bathroom and into my room, where I grab the first clothes I see. Three sides of the cube that is my room are completely black now. There's water oozing out of the ceiling and dripping down. The smell is powerfully strong.

I step into some shorts, not caring if they're as rank as the room they've been lying in, and I'm down the stairs in four leaps. I scrabble in my wet coat pocket for the phone, and dial Neisha's number, aware of Mum and Debbie standing in the doorway of the lounge watching me. It rings for ages.

'Come on. Come on.'

Mum's got that look again, the one where she's trying not to show me that she thinks I've gone crazy.

At last Neisha's voice. 'Hello? Dad, is that you? Dad, I'm scared. The taps are all running. I can't turn them off. There's water outside. The river—'

'Neisha, it's me. Carl. Listen, you've got to—'

'Carl?'

The phone goes dead. She's hung up. The moment she knew it was me, she hung up. She still hates me. But what was she saying? The taps … the river …

'Shit.' He's coming to get her.

'Mum,' I say, 'Mum, she won't listen to me. You've got to speak to her. Tell her—' Tell her what? To stay in the house? To try and get out now, go somewhere else? 'Tell her to keep dry.'

'What? Carl, slow down. Everything's all right.'

'It's important, Mum. She's not safe. He's going to get her. He's going to kill her, Mum. You've got to ring her. Please, Mum. Please.' I can hear myself babbling. I can hear how mad it sounds.

'Carl, you don't need to worry. She won't go out in this, will she? It's horrible.'

'But it's not safe for her inside or out. She needs to keep dry.'

Now Debbie chips in.

'Kerry, first he's scared of getting wet. Next he's hitting you. Then he's stripping off in the middle of the rec. Now he doesn't want this girl to get wet. Can't you hear how … how odd that sounds? Can't you?'

'Debbie, I've told you, I'm dealing with it. Let's just get the funeral over with and …'

This is just wasting time, when there's no time to waste.

'Mum, it's life or death. Ring her. Please ring her.' I thrust the phone towards her.

'Carl, I don't know what's gone on between you two, but she doesn't need any more aggro at the moment. It's the funeral tomorrow. Leave her be now. Just leave her be.'

'You're not going to ring her?'

'No.'

'For Christ's sake!'

Still holding the phone I slam out of the house. I'm only wearing a pair of shorts, nothing on my feet, but I don't care. The rain's thundering down. I run along the walkway and fly over the concrete wall, landing squarely on my feet, ignoring the pain that shoots up my bare legs.

No one's playing by the garages today. The yard is covered by a sheet of water, the surface dancing under the onslaught of rain. In the middle, water bubbles up through a grating, playing keepy-uppy with a crumpled plastic football which bobs up and down, unable to break away.

I run on, getting colder and wetter as my feet pound through the surface water. It's only when I've gone past the rec and I'm diving down the alleyways leading to Neisha's that the images really register: sand bags, surface water, a football dancing. Water bubbling up.

All this time, I've been terrified of water falling on me – I forgot about it creeping up, rising, flooding.

Still running, I redial Neisha's number.

She answers immediately.

'Carl? Carl! Help me!'

She's terrified.

'What's happening, Neisha?' I gasp, trying to get enough breath to speak. 'Are you okay?'

'I'm trapped. The water's a foot deep outside. It's starting to come in under the door. All the taps are running brown. I can't stop them. I—'

'It's okay. It's okay. Where are you now?'

'I'm downstairs, in the hall.'

'Go upstairs. Can you do that? Just go upstairs. Keep out of the water. Keep dry. I'll be there in five minutes.'

She starts screaming. I can't hear any words, just the raw one-pitch note of her terror. I'm yelling now, trying to get her to tell me what's happening.

'Neisha! Neisha!'

'Oh my God, the toilet's flooding! There's stuff … there's sewage coming up! Oh God! Oh God!'

'Neisha, go upstairs! Go now! Please. I'm nearly with you. Just go upstairs. I'm going to stay on the phone. Tell me when you're there.'

I clamp the phone to my ear and peg it down the road. A series of sirens wails from somewhere across town. I'm nearly at the bridge. I can't see the arches any more – the river is up to the level of the road. There are cars pulled up on either side, a police car blocking the entrance with its lights flashing. A copper in a fluorescent jacket is putting out yellow cones.

A cluster of onlookers is gathered along the water's edge – it's way over both banks.

'The bridge is closed, mate,' one of them says to me. 'There are cracks in the tarmac. It's going to go.' He's got his camera at the ready. One for the album.

I carry on running and try to dodge past the copper. 'Oi! Slow down. You can't go over there,' he shouts, lunging towards me and catching my arm.

I wrestle myself free, losing the phone as I do so. It slips out of my fingers and plops into the ankle-deep water.

I leave PC Plod behind and run on to the bridge. The road rises out of the flood as I reach its humped back. And now I can see that everyone's right. The surface under my feet is tearing apart. There's a crack right across the middle. I can feel it moving and I run faster, so my feet are hardly touching the ground. I'm heading down the other side, back into the floodwater. There's a soft noise behind me, a slurping, slushing sound, almost a sigh. A chorus of shouts goes up. I'm on the other bank now and I glance behind.

One side of the bridge has gone, collapsed into the swirling river, just a gap where the road should be. Another second and I would have gone with it.

I'm not far from Neisha's now. The townscape's utterly changed. Half the familiar landmarks have disappeared. Kingsleigh's a series of islands occupied by houses and trees.

I'm wading through knee-deep water. It's cold and thick and brown. I can't see what's under the surface. Each step forward is a step into the unknown. I try to follow the line of the road, trusting my instinct. The ground slopes down and the water travels further up my legs. The water's not still, it's flowing, and the movement is surprisingly strong. It's buffeting against me and now I'm glad I'm not wearing trousers – there's nothing extra to drag in the current. I'm moving with the flow, which should be easy, shouldn't it? But when I lift one foot up, the water tries to push it forward, suck it away from me. It feels like there's someone in there, pulling at me, trying to have me over. I peer at the water around me. It's so muddy I can't see past the surface. Is Rob down there?

My foot searches for solid ground, toes clawing at the unseen lumps and bumps. I'm losing my nerve – I have to plant it down firmly, believe that there's something there to plant it on.

There are other people wading through the water, making their way out of the cottages, heading for higher ground. One guy's carrying a toddler on his shoulders. She's laughing, patting his head like this is all a game. He's grim-faced, holding on to her legs. He shouts at her to sit still. Her face changes as he grips harder and she starts to cry.

The guy shouts over to me.

'It's rising too fast. Go back, son.'

I look past him to the terrace of houses beyond. The water is up to the downstairs windows. Did Neisha make it upstairs?

'I've got to get in there,' I shout back. 'My friend's in there.'

He shakes his head, and struggles on.

I'm opposite the house now. The garden wall is somewhere under the surface. I edge forward, anxious not to clatter into it, trip over it, cut myself open.

The water's up to my waist.

A branch a couple of metres long is floating towards

me. I grab it and use it as a probe, poking it into the water ahead. I find the wall and manage to clamber over. Something tears at the skin on my legs. I think of Rob's nails, the mud caked underneath them, but I keep going, ditching the branch so I can use my hands to paddle through the water. I'm still on my feet, but only just. It's almost chest height here.

'Carl!'

I look up. Neisha's at the top window. It's open and she's leaning out.

'Get in,' I yell, waving my arms at her. 'Keep dry.'

'What?' She doesn't move. Instead, she's craning forward.

'What's that in the water?' she shouts.

I look round. I can't see anything apart from the branch I chucked away and that's rapidly floating off past the houses.

'Nothing,' I shout back.

'In the water behind you. What is it?'

I check again. Apart from the people making their way out of the flood, I'm on my own. Maybe it's a trick of the light on the water or something. Maybe there's some debris that I can't see.

'I'm stuck, Carl. I can't get out. The water's coming up the stairs. Should I jump?'

'For Christ's sake, stay there! You'll be okay. I'll try and find my way in.'

She leans forward, further out into the rain.

'Get back in!' I scream. 'Get back in! I'm coming to get you.'

I wade to the front of the house, using my arms to get me through the water. I look through the lounge window. A coffee table is floating forlornly in the middle of the room. The water level seems slightly lower than outside, but it's at least half a metre. The window is old-style, the sort where the bottom half slides up. Used to be Rob's favourite kind. Much easier to break into than modern double-glazed plastic jobs. Trouble is, I'm not at a great angle here for getting a purchase on anything. I have a go with one, but I can't get it to budge. I'm cursing myself for letting the branch go. I could have used it to lever the window up or smash my way in.

I look around but there's nothing useful floating anywhere near now. Then I remember that there were some stone pots of flowers near the front door. They're underwater now, but I've got a good idea where they are. I reckon one of them would do the business.

'Carl! Carl! What are you doing?'

Neisha's leaning right out now, craning to see me.

'I'm going to get one of those pots, smash the window.'

'Don't do that! Dad'll go mad. Maybe I can let you in. I could try the door. I'll come down.'

'No! Don't come into the water. Neisha, please. Stay where you are. For God's sake, get your head in. Keep dry!'

I edge my way to the right, holding on to the front wall, feeling for the pots with my feet. My toe hits something hard. I take a breath, duck under the surface and reach for the pot. It's really heavy and I can't get a good

236

grip on it. It moves a little but not enough. The water over my head is freaking me out. I'm trying desperately not to think of that other time, but I can't help it.

A confusion of arms and legs, hands and feet, all mixed up in the water. He must have taken his hands off her because he punches me in the face, then he grips my neck and squeezes. He forces my head under the water. I panic and lash out, trying to hit, scratch, tear, kick – anything that will make him let go.

I stand up and flick the water out of my hair, rub my hands across my eyes. For a moment I don't know where I am. I stand and suck air into my lungs. Then I remember – this isn't a nightmare, it isn't a dream. The river is flooding. Neisha's in danger.

'Are you okay?' she shouts down.

She's leaning way over the window ledge now. Her wet hair falls forward like a curtain either side of her face.

'It's heavy, that's all.'

'You can do it between you. The two of you could manage.'

'What?' She's not making any sense.

'You can do it together. You and ... you and whoever's behind ... oh my God. No, no, no!' She's staring at the water behind me.

'No, no, no! Oh my God, oh my God.'

She's terrified of something she's seen down in the murk. Rob? I look round wildly, but there's nothing there.

She's gone back into her room, like I wanted her to, like I kept telling her to – but her face, the last glimpse I got before she retreated, was a picture of horror. Is Rob here? Can she see him? But how is that possible? She's never been able to see him before.

If I was scared before, it's ten times worse now. I've got to get in there. She needs me.

I take a deep breath and go under again, bending right down so that I can get a better grip and use my legs more in the lift. And now the pot shifts. I take the weight of it squarely in both hands, push up with my legs and I'm there. I stagger through the water to the window, grunting with the effort. This is a one-shot deal. Trying to keep some momentum going I thrust the pot up and away from me with every ounce of strength that I've got left. It thuds against the glass but doesn't go through. It drops into the water and I leap back so it doesn't land on my feet.

'Shit!'

I'm gasping for breath, disappointed and angry at my failure. I look at the window again, and see that the glass is cracked. I'm halfway there, I just need something else to finish the job. I bunch my fist up and wonder if I can do it on my own. I need something to wrap round to protect it, stop myself slicing an artery open – the only thing I've got is my shorts …

Without warning, there's a sharp pain in my shoulder. I turn my head. There's a wooden chair barrelling over in the water next to me and I'm bleeding from a nasty flesh wound.

'I've called the police!' Neisha shouts. 'I've called my dad! They're all coming, so you'd better get out of here!'

It was her, she threw the chair.

'Get out! Get out now!'

'I'm trying to help you!'

'You filthy lying tosser, Carl Adams! Fuck off! Fuck off before they arrest you!'

She's gone mad. But there's no time to reason with her. She's given me the tool I need to get into the house, and I've got to get to her before Rob does.

I grab the chair and swing it above my head, aiming at the cracked glass. It smashes and I'm in. Above me, Neisha's screaming at the top of her voice. Something else comes flying through the air and plops into the water a few centimetres behind me.

I put my hands on the window ledge, checking quickly for jagged glass, and, with a little jump, I bring my legs up to perch on the edge. I launch myself into the lounge and wade through the water across the room to the hall. Except it's not just water. There are bits of paper and all sorts of debris mixed up in it. I try not to think what else in is there. I look up instead of down, expecting to see Neisha at the top of the stairs, but she isn't there.

The house is eerily quiet. Water slops gently against the stairs. Furniture thuds softly against wallpaper. Rain patters on the windows.

'Neisha?' I shout.

No answer.

The silence makes this whole thing feel wrong, like I shouldn't be here. But I'm here to save her, I tell myself. I'm here to be the hero she thought I was.

'Neisha?'

I glance round. Still no Rob. I'm at the bottom of the stairs now. I start climbing up, emerging from the water step by step. I nearly bust a gut to get here, but now I'm creeped out. My heart's beating like mad in my chest. I'm straining my eyes and ears for some clue as to what's going on. My legs are scratched and bleeding. There's blood dripping down my chest, too, from the cut on my shoulder.

At the top of the stairs I hesitate. She was in the front bedroom when she was shouting at me. She must still be in there ...

'Neisha, it's me. Carl. Where are you?'

I turn back on myself and start padding along the landing. The doors are all open except the one to her room, and I peer in as I pass. They're empty, each room as beautifully neat and clean as the next. Up here, there's no sign of the carnage outside and downstairs. It's bizarre that somewhere can look so normal when only a few metres away the world's being swallowed up, wrecked, changed for ever.

I'm dripping on to the carpet, leaving wet, bloody footprints in the soft pile. On the scale of things, it doesn't matter, but it adds to my unease, the sense that I've got no right to be here, that I'm trespassing, spoiling things.

I stop in front of the door to Neisha's room and knock, gently, calling out her name.

There's no response. I reach for the handle, turn it and inch the door open.

I can't see her. The window is open and I can hear the wind and rain outside, but nothing inside. It's almost like the room's holding its breath. I push the door open wider and step in.

There's a flash of recognition. I've seen this room

before. The bed. It's where the photos were taken. It's where—

Something hits me on the side of the head. Everything turns red, then black, as pain explodes inside my skull. I stagger to the side but manage to stay on my feet and as my vision starts to clear, I'm hit again, this time across the top of my back, catapulting me forwards. I put my hands out to break my fall and crunch down on the carpet next to her bed.

'I told you to fuck off!'

Holding my hand to the side of my face, I twist round and look up. Neisha's standing a couple of metres away from me, holding the metal stand of a bedside light as if it was a baseball bat. She sweeps it through the air in front of her, frowning with the effort, swiping it from side to side like a kid fighting Darth Maul with a toy light sabre.

'Jesus, Neisha!'

She turns her attention back to me, raises the lamp up again, steps forward and brings it down on my side with full force, knocking the breath out of me.

'I don't want you here! Either of you. Get out! Get out!'

I move my arm to try and shield as much of my head as I can. 'Okay, okay,' I yell. 'I'll get out. I can't if you keep hitting me though. Give me a freakin' chance.'

I start crawling towards the door, watching her feet retreat, keeping her distance from me now. In the doorway, I stop.

'What have you seen, Neisha? Is it Rob? Look, you asked me to help you. That's why I'm here.'

'You lying bastard!' She's shouting at me, spit coming

out of her mouth as she does. 'You said you'd changed, but you've been lying to me the whole time.' Her eyes are wide and wild, the muscles in her arms tense, veins standing out like whipcords. 'Why did you bring him here, Carl? Why would you do that to me again? I was ready to trust you.'

'Tell me what you've seen, Neisha. I didn't bring anyone. It's just me.'

She steps forward again, and I stop crawling and cower closer to the floor, bringing my knees up to my chest.

'You're lying! He's there!' She points wildly to a patch of thin air. 'That bastard brother of yours. He's there, right next to you. At least, he was. I … I can't see him now. Where's he gone? Oh God, where is he?' She twirls round, sweeping the lamp through three hundred and sixty degrees. 'He was here, I swear he was.'

'He was here. And now he isn't.' The penny drops. 'You're drying off.'

'What?' she says.

'You see him when you're wet. Like I did, but I don't see him at all now. I can't see him. He disappeared earlier. He's come to you instead. That's why I rang you. I worked it out …'

She's still holding the lamp like a weapon. She narrows her eyes.

'What did you see, Carl? Tell me again.'

'Rob. Only Rob like he was when he drowned. He just had his shorts on,' – suddenly I'm very aware of how I'm dressed, or not dressed – 'nothing else. Very pale, and streaked with—'

'—mud,' she says. 'Look at you, Carl. Look at you. You're just like him. But you've got blood … What are you playing at?'

'I can explain.' I sit up a bit, still ready to curl up if she gets nasty again. 'I was in the bath when I twigged what was going on. He wasn't there, you see. I was completely wet and he wasn't there. And suddenly I realised he'd be here.'

The lamp hangs by her side now. She looks at me still grovelling on the floor, and it feels like she's come back to me.

'God, Carl, I never really actually believed you. All that time, I thought you were losing it. I'm so sorry. What's he going to do, Carl? What's he going to do to me?'

There's no easy way to say this. I get to my feet. I want to walk over to her. I want to hold her hand or wrap my arms round her, but I don't want to push it. She was beating me hard a few minutes ago. So I stand where I am, near the doorway, and I tell her.

'He wants to kill you, Neisha. I wouldn't help him, so he's going to try to do it himself. But I won't let him. I won't, Neisha.'

She sinks on to the bed, perching on the edge, and puts the lamp down next to her.

'He's going to drown me.'

She looks strangely calm, but her voice is unsteady, giving away how she really feels. And now I do move. I sit next to her and, without thinking, put my arm round her shoulders.

'But he can't hurt you,' I say. 'Not if you stay out of the

243

water. That's what I was trying to say on the phone.'

I lean my head against hers. She squeals, then hisses, 'He's here. Carl, Carl, he's here.'

What was I thinking? My skin is wet. My hair is wet. I jump up, away from her.

'Wipe your face,' I bark. 'Quickly, wipe it on the bedspread. I'm sorry. I just wanted to be close to you. That was my fault. I'm soaked. I'm sorry, I'm sorry.'

'For God's sake. Do you want to bring him back again?' She lifts one edge of the bedcover and dries herself, her actions jerky and panicky. Then she scans the room. 'One minute I think I can trust you, and the next ...'

'I know. I'm sorry. I just forgot. You *can* trust me, Neisha, I swear. I won't let him win. I won't let anyone hurt you ever again. Has he gone?'

She looks at me hard for a moment, assessing me with her big brown eyes. Then she turns and looks around the room.

'Yes,' she says. 'He's gone. I'll get a towel from the bathroom. You shut the window. Shut him out.'

I cross to the window. Outside, the water is higher now. It can't keep on rising for ever, though, can it? It'll have to stop sometime.

I heave on the window and pull it down. It slides shut and I press on the frame and twist the lock round to make sure nothing can come in. Rain spatters against the glass, but it can't hurt us now.

Neisha's back, carrying a couple of towels and some clothes. She stands in the doorway, and I feel self-conscious – her fully clothed and me with hardly a stitch

244

on. My arms and legs are skinny, a boy's arms and legs, not a man's. But I don't feel like a boy when I look at her.

I catch her looking me up and down. Up to my face and down to my—

'Here,' she says, and throws the bundle of towels and clothes towards me. I catch them in both arms and dump them on her bed.

'Ta,' I say. I'm blushing and it's a relief to bury my face in a towel for a moment, try and get myself back together.

'They're my dad's clothes, but, you know, better than nothing ...'

I dive into a yellow polo shirt, put a thick fleece on top. My shorts are still dripping.

'You can finish changing in the bathroom,' she says. 'I found you some jeans. I wasn't sure about pants ...'

I swipe the jeans off the bed.

'That's cool,' I say. 'I really couldn't wear your dad's pants, even if my life depended on it.'

Her face slowly breaks into a smile, then she grins.

'I know. Eww.'

In the bathroom, I quickly peel off my shorts, dry myself and put the jeans on. They're way too big, but they'll do. I'm already feeling warmer. I shuffle out of the bathroom and look over the banister. The water's about halfway up the stairs now, lapping at the hall wallpaper. I stare for a minute or so, trying to see whether it's creeping upwards, but it's moving too much for me to be able to judge.

It's going to be okay. All we have to do is sit it out. It's a bit like being on a desert island, and I can't think of anyone I'd rather be here with than Neisha.

I'm about to pad back along the landing when I look up. She's coming towards me.

'Wondered where you'd got to,' she says. 'Oh God, you look … weird … in my dad's clothes, I mean. Not a good look. At least you're dry, I s'pose.'

She puts her hands on my waist. I mirror her. We hesitate, awkward for a moment, then she slides her arms round me, drawing me close, and hugs me.

I kiss the side of her face, not much more than a peck, but then she turns and our mouths meet and we kiss silently and tenderly. Below us, the hall table taps gently against the wall.

We draw apart. I hold her face with both my hands.

'Neisha,' I say. 'I'm so, so sorry. For everything.'

'It's all right,' she says. 'You don't need to say it.'

'Yeah, I do. It's important. I'm sorry for the things I did. I've done some terrible, terrible things.'

'It's okay,' she says. She brings her finger up to my lips. 'Shh. I know.'

I open my lips and the end of her finger crooks into my mouth. I kiss it, then take both her hands and hold them between us.

'I want to say it. If I don't say it, then it's not real. Now, or afterwards. I need to say the words and you need to hear them. God, I'm crap at this. I wish I could say what I really feel.'

'You're not crap. Go on.'

Her face is serious now. She's listening carefully and

there's something so trusting about her expression, even after everything we've been through.

'I can't make everything right,' I say, 'but maybe I can start to make things better. I did something so bad that by rights you should hate me, and I know you did for a while. I'll do anything to make it up to you. I'll spend the rest of my life trying to make you forget, forgive.'

'The rest of your life?' she says. 'Are you asking me to marry you, 'cos that's way out there …'

There's a hint of a smile at the corners of her mouth and I feel like I'm stuffing up, messing up this opportunity big style. This time, this moment, is slipping away from me. I look up to the ceiling.

'God, I'm not doing this very well. I told you I was crap.'

'No, you're not. Sorry, I'm listening.' She strokes my face.

'I'm not asking you to marry me, but I do love you, Neisha. That's all. I love you.'

I want her to say it back, really quickly, like she doesn't have to think about it at all.

But she doesn't.

My heart's sinking inside. I'm ashamed and embarrassed at what I just said. But then she kisses me again, and it's tender and sweet, full of comfort and warmth. And maybe it doesn't matter if she won't say it, can't say it, yet.

When we stop kissing, I hold her close.

'I'm scared,' she says.

'I think the water's stopped rising,' I say. 'I think we're going to be okay.'

247

And then all around us the windows burst and the world turns dark. The water rushes in, sweeping her out of my arms.

TWENTY-EIGHT

No time to take a breath. No time to say, 'Hold on.'

The water is sudden and brutal, cutting my legs from under me, flipping me over, throwing me against a wall or a banister or a ceiling, I can't tell. I can't fight it – I don't know how. Which way is up? What do I cling to? The water is everywhere, dragging on my clothes. I twist and turn, helpless. I'm slammed into something else. I try to grip on to it, but my scrabbling fingers can't find anything to hold.

My mouth's full of water. I try to spit it out, using the small pockets of air left inside me to push the stuff out, and then I realise how stupid that is. My lungs are empty now and my brain is telling me to breathe in. I fight the urge to open my mouth again, but the instinct is too strong. Moving makes it worse, so I freeze and as I do so, my body finds its way up, only now up is actually sideways. I break the surface and twist my head to the left, gulping at the air. Everything hurts. I use my first lungful to try and get rid of the water still in my pipes, breathing in hard, breathing out hard too. Another breath in and I force air out of my nose. How can water hurt so much?

Neisha's not here.

I drop my legs down, tread water and try to suss out where I am. There are maybe ten centimetres or so between the top of my head and the ceiling. The room I'm in is quite small and by the look of the light fitting in the middle, I'm in the bathroom.

Don't think about drains. Don't think about sewage. Find Neisha. That's all. Find her.

She's not in here, not on the surface anyway.

'I hate my face in the water ...'

The water's six or seven feet deep in this room, but out in the hallway it will be twice that, more. Oh God, where is she?

She must have been blasted in the same direction as me, surely? I take another breath and drop under the surface, sinking down so that my feet touch the floor, paddling with my hands, turning and looking. A little light comes in from the bathroom window, highlighting the white fittings – the bath, the sink, the toilet – through the dirty water. I keep thinking of a ship, the Titanic or something, sunk to the bottom of the sea. But this isn't a ship, it's a house, a house like I've never seen one before.

She's not here. I push off from the floor and bob up by the ceiling to get some more air. A big breath and I'm down again, this time swimming under the door frame onto the landing. I try to get the map of her house straight in my head. The bathroom is next to her room at the front of the house. If she was washed in the same direction as me, then she'll either be in the bedroom next door or in the hallway.

I surface again, scanning around for any sign of her. There's a layer of debris floating on the top now. I gasp as I catch sight of a child, floating face down a couple of metres away. I swim over and flip it over, crying out as the face turns towards me. The eyes are criss—crosses of thread, the hair is sodden wool. Not a child, a big cloth doll. Repulsed, I drop it and swim away.

I stop to call out.

'Neisha? Neisha?'

And then I realise that my head is almost touching the ceiling. The water's rising. Time's running out.

Another breath and I duck under the door frame into the front bedroom, her room, frogging with my legs to swim lower in the water, looking left and right. I swim to the front wall and my hands find glass. The window is still closed. If I open it, will it let some of this water out … or let more water in? I peer at the window. It's all one colour, grey from the bottom to the top of the glass. There's a wall of water outside. It's deeper out there, and it's still trying to push its way in.

I turn around and head back again. The pressure is building in my lungs, so I make for the surface, but as my head erupts from the water it brushes something hard. There are only a few centimetres between the surface of the water and the ceiling now, and that will be gone soon. Shit!

If she isn't here, then she must be somewhere in the hallway. Unless the water funnelled round. Could it have hit the front of the house and washed backwards?

I don't know what to do. Should I search the other bedrooms? Or dive down? If she's been taken to one of the rooms downstairs, she's got no chance. Taken ... taken by the water. Taken by Rob. I can't see him, but I know that he's here. He's here with her and she must be terrified.

I've hardly got any time at all to find her and get her out. No more dithering, I'll just have to try somewhere. Anywhere. Think, Carl, think. If Rob's here, in the water, he'll have taken her to the worst place, the deepest, the most difficult to get out of.

I suck in another lungful of air, trying not to wonder if it will be my last. I jackknife forwards and dive down. There are strange currents at work. As I scoop the water below me, I'm drawn away from the front of the house towards the back. It's taking all my strength to move downwards and I find myself moving with the flow. I'm in the downstairs hallway now and things close in as I'm carried away from the stairwell and under the hall ceiling. It feels like an underwater tunnel. It feels like I'll never get out again.

I'm trying to hold the air in, but it's got a life of its own. The surface is a long way up, and it wants to get there. I let a little out of my nose. The bubbles trail past my face on their way up. I must hold the rest in, but it's pushing at my throat, trying to force its way out.

Through stinging eyes I can see there are three door-ways ahead. One in front, and one either side. I haven't got time to check them all. The air finally finds its escape, bursting out of my mouth, filling the water with bubbles. I put my hand out to try and catch them and then I watch them dance away, and it's almost like they're nothing to do with me. This body isn't mine any more. I'm watching, just watching.

All I need to do is take a deep breath in and it will all be over. I'm scared, but not for myself. It's all about Neisha.

I'm suspended in the water. I'm empty and soon I'll be full. Isn't my life meant to flash before me now? It doesn't. I don't see anything. I just feel sorry. I let her down. I failed her. Again.

Suddenly to my left, there's movement. Something dark coming towards me in the water. Hands out in front, feet kicking behind, long hair swaying like seaweed around her face. Neisha?

It is her! She's moving fast. She smiles and slips past me, easing her way back along the hallway and then up and up into the stairwell. I twist in the water and follow. My head hits the ceiling before I break the surface. I turn my face sideways and my mouth finds the tiny layer of air still left. A couple of centimetres. No more. I'm almost kissing the plaster but I'm breathing. For now, I'm breathing.

I turn my head to find Neisha. She's under the surface, treading water. I don't understand why she isn't gasping for air like me. She smiles again and turns away, swimming against the flow.

The window in the back bedroom is gone, blown inwards by the torrent of water. It's still pouring in but the current isn't as strong any more. Neisha swims through. I'm right behind her. We're out.

We're swimming towards the light, and this time as I surface, there's bright sky above me. There's a break in the clouds and the sun's shining on the water. The contrast is too much. For a moment I'm blinded.

I shield my eyes and look for Neisha. I bob along like a cork, twisting round to try and spot her. She must be close – she was right in front of me after all. Where is she? We're behind the row of houses and we're part of the swollen, flooded river, being carried downstream. Except it's not 'we', I'm on my own. I can't see Neisha anywhere.

There are shouts from the edge of the water, twenty yards away. I look up. People are pointing at me and waving.

And then I hear her.

'I love you, Carl.'

Her voice is close. I swivel round, but I can't see her.

'Neisha? Neisha!'

'I forgive you. I love you. Goodbye.'

I feel her breath in my ear, smell a whiff of honey and vanilla. And then it's gone.

My brain's working so slowly. Maybe it's the cold. Maybe I'm waterlogged.

Since when did she learn to swim like that? Why wasn't she gulping for air back in the house?

Because that wasn't Neisha.

It was part of her, the part released from her body when it died.

Because she drowned in the house, in that room downstairs.

'No! No, no, please God, no!'

There's no point looking for her here, in this fat, swollen sea of water, snaking its way through the rooftops. She's gone.

Rob won. I wouldn't bring her to the water, so he brought the water to her.

I look behind me. I'm about ten metres past the end of the row and moving further away. My body's low in the water, dragged down by my clothes. Maybe I should let the water take me. What's the point of carrying on? I've lost my brother. I've lost my girl. I had hardly anything in my life and now there's nothing left.

The water tugs at me, pulling me down. My mouth dips under the surface, then my nose. It would be so easy to let go now, to let this happen. And why wouldn't I?

As my ears go under, I hear another voice. Not words this time, a low, grating laugh. Rob. He's not urging me on any more. He's not threatening. He doesn't need to. It's over.

I wasn't smart enough, or quick enough, or strong enough to save her.

She got what she deserved.

He's gloating. I close my eyes. I don't want to see his face again. I don't want to see anything.

Something lands in the water, splashing the top of my face. I push down with my hands to peek above the surface. A large orange plastic ring is floating a metre or so away from me.

'Grab it. Grab it, son!'

There are people screaming at me. They've thrown me a lifebelt. Instinct kicks in and I thrash my legs and reach forward. I manage to grab one side.

'Get your arms through and we'll pull you in!'

I duck under and come up inside the ring. There's a cheer as I ease my head and shoulders in and rest my elbows either side of me. The river pulls against me, but I'm not moving any more. The ring is attached to a rope and now people are starting to pull me upstream. I'm getting closer to the row of terraced houses, and as I draw level with the end one, I think of Neisha's body, trapped somewhere inside, at the mercy of the freezing water, and I can't bear it.

I let her down, but I can do one last thing for her. I'll bring her out.

Still propped up, I wriggle out of my jeans. I cross my arms over my body and hold my polo shirt either side. Then I lift my arms above my head, peel the shirt off and slip out of the ring, back down into the water.

TWENTY-NINE

Out of the ring, I'm battling against the current. I front-crawl my way towards the houses, but it's a struggle even without waterlogged clothes. My plan is to swim to the house and duck under the water near the broken window, but I'm so tired. The worst thing is, I can't work out exactly where Neisha's house is. The water is just below the roofs. Then I twig that you can tell where one house joins on to the next, where the drainpipe joins the gutter. Neisha's house should be three from the end. I plough upstream towards it.

I swim up to the building, hold on to some guttering and take a few moments to get myself together. The plastic I'm gripping bends and strains. From across the water, people are shouting. Someone let out a wail of anguish when I left the lifesaving ring. Now they're yelling at me to stay where I am, hold on until a boat can reach me.

If I can get Neisha out, I'll get her body on to the roof, rather than try to swim anywhere with it. *When*, not if. I'm going to do it. I owe her.

I take a quick look around. The sunlight is still hitting the water. I can feel its warmth on my shoulders and just for a moment I'm back with Neisha at the playground, and she's kissing me, and the warmth from her skin and the warmth from the sun are part of the same thing. She holds me, wraps her arms and legs round me, makes me topple over, makes me laugh.

I'll never have that again.

The shock of realisation is like the stab of a blade. It cuts me in two, skewers me, takes my breath away. But I need my breath. I need it one last time – to go and fetch her. She can't hold me again, but I can hold her.

I wonder if the water's stopped rising now the rain has stopped. How long will it take to sink back down, for the world to be back to how it should be? I wonder if I'll see it, and I realise I don't care either way. The world will never be back to how it should be. Neisha's dead. Nothing will ever be the same again.

Come on. Do it. Do it now.

I push my diaphragm down into my guts, force my ribs out and up, and suck air smoothly into my lungs. It might be my last breath. So be it.

I sink into the water, using my hands against the brick to guide myself to her bedroom window. I grip the frame either side and brace against it, propelling myself in. Panic flutters in my stomach as I think about how far I've got to swim, how far down I've got to go. The further I get from the window, the worse it gets. There's no surface here, only water above and below and around me. I feel its weight, feel the pressure of the walls and ceiling. But I can't let that stop me. I've got to keep calm. I've got to focus on swimming, nothing else.

I'm through her room and out into the landing. Now down. I squeeze my fingers together and scoop the water, pushing it behind me, pulling myself forward. I kick my legs breast-stroke style as I dive down, down, down, past the banisters and the pictures that still cling crazily to the wall. I sweep debris aside: pages from magazines, little cane baskets, birthday cards, paperback books. The stuff that made this house a proper home, the normal things that people take for granted. I bat them out of the way and swim down the hall.

It's quiet here. The only noise comes from me – the busy, rippling, chuckling sound of air escaping from my mouth. The pressure's building inside me. I clamp my lips shut and it's eerily quiet again. I'm close to the doorway, the one I saw Neisha swim out of. I'm scared, but I want to see her again. I want that more than anything in the world.

I kick my legs again, and I'm in. It is, was, a dining room. A table's floating madly on its side somewhere near the ceiling. China plates and cups lie shattered on the floor.

There are two bodies in the room.

They hang vertically in the water, like a pair of broken puppets.

One dark. One pale.

Neisha is wearing her jeans and hoodie, heavy clothes, the clothes that helped to kill her. Her hair dances around her head like a black halo. Her eyes and mouth are open. She looks surprised. No. Terrified.

The body next to her has its back to me – head down, arms by its sides, naked apart from some boxers. Pale flesh, streaked with mud.

Neisha sways gently to the rhythm of the water, trapped in a silent disco. But it's not silent here. There's a voice, filling the room, the house, my head.

I knew you'd come.

Slowly, the second body starts to move, hands jerking upwards, body twisting round and, finally, the face turns towards me. His eyes are black holes of pain, his mouth a dark slash across his face, stretched in a hideous smile.

I scream, the noise distorted by the water, bubbles bursting out of me, filling the space around my head.

Rob's mouth opens wider and he tips his head back and laughs.

And now, as the last bubble of air leaves me, I finally get it. I thought he wanted to kill Neisha. He was threatening me to get to her. But that was only half the game. He wanted me too. All along, he knew he was going to kill me.

My stomach contracts. I'm empty.

He's watching me, savouring my last moments.

I need to finish the job.

He's done it. The job's finished. I stare at his face, waiting for him to disappear, for this all to be over. His eyes aren't black any more, they're burning with a strange cold light that's almost too bright to look at. But I can't look away.

So this is how it ends. Me and him. It was always me and him. Him and me. Rob and Carl.

Until Neisha. She changed everything.

He's making me forget about Neisha.

I don't want to die looking at him.

I don't want to die. Not yet. Not like this.

I came here to fetch her. That's why I'm here; it's flooding back to me now. I'm not dead yet, and I can still do this last thing for her.

I want to breathe in, but I'm not going to. I bite hard, clenching my jaw shut, tensing every muscle in my face. I'm not going to breathe in.

The French windows are open, the catch broken by the force of the water. I can just make out the outline of a brick barbeque, the squares of patio tiles. And beyond, a thin strand of light filtering down, with the promise of air and sun.

I launch myself at Neisha, locking my arms under hers, pulling her towards the opening. I'm down to my last ounce of strength, but I'm going to use it to bust us out of here.

Rob roars in my ears.

It's over! It's over, Cee!

He darts in front of me, swirling round and round, screaming on the inside of my skull.

But he can't stop me. It's over, he's won, but it's going to be over the way I choose.

We're through the French windows. I can't kick my legs any more. There's no oxygen in my body – it's all used up. All I can do is hold on to her.

It's me and her. Neisha and me. And it's not an unhappy ending, after all. We're together – floating, twisting, twirling together – and eventually we'll find the surface, and the sun will touch our faces again, breathe on our skin, kiss us one last time.

THIRTY

I open my eyes. There's stuff in my mouth. I turn my head and spit.

There's a face a metre from mine, sideways on. Hair plastered onto her forehead. Full lips slightly apart. Warm, honey-coloured skin. Eyes closed, stubby eyelashes clumped with water.

The face is moving, rocking backwards and forwards, pivoting on the back of the head where it touches the ground.

The movement stops.

A man leans over her. He tilts her head back and lifts her chin. Then he pinches her nose and leans further over and kisses her. He pulls away, takes a deep breath and kisses her again.

I feel sick. He's violating her. Neisha, my girl. Right in

front of me.

'Get off!' I shout, but it's only in my head. My lips don't move. All I can do is watch.

He stops and sits back on his heels. Now he bunches up his hands, puts one on top of the other and presses them onto the middle of her chest, pushing so hard that her whole body moves, her head rocking backwards and forwards.

He's trying to save her.

He's sweating with the effort. The sun's beating down and steam rises up from the wet ground around me, but I can only feel the warmth on my face, prickling my wet skin. I look down. I'm covered with a layer of coats.

Someone squeezes my hand.

'What's your name, son?' A woman's voice.

I can't remember. I can only remember the girl's name. My girl's name. Neisha. I turn my head back to her.

'Don't worry,' the woman says, squeezing my hand again. 'The ambulance will be here soon. It's going to be all right.'

Neisha's head rocks backwards and forwards. Her eyes are closed.

'It's all right. It's going to be all right.'

THIRTY-ONE

I've never been to a funeral before.

There are more people here than I thought there'd be, but as we wait for it to start all I can think about is the people who aren't here.

I sit at the front with Mum and Auntie Debbie. I've come straight from hospital in some clothes the social worker there found me. It's not cold here, but I'm shivering and sweating. The cuts on my legs and shoulder have started to go bad. They've given me some antibiotics but I guess they haven't kicked in yet. I wipe my face with a hankie.

'You all right?' Mum says. She's looking like death herself.

'Yeah,' I say. 'It's just—'

I stop. The double doors are opening. The coffin's

coming in. A shiny wooden box, carried by six blokes in dark suits.

Mum starts to cry.

'I can't do this. I can't—'

I start to put my arm round her, but on the other side Debbie's already got her, holding her tight, pulling her away from me. And so I sit, on my own, and watch them carry him in.

The hairs on the back of my neck are standing up.

I'm scared. Scared of this place, the way everything's happening around us, like a well-oiled machine. The end of the line, it's happening and we can't stop it.

I'm thinking that it could have been me inside that box. First at the lake, and then at Neisha's house. I've come close. Really close. And one day it will be me. And maybe that's what I'm scared of. The end. My end. There's no escape.

The service starts and I follow what everyone else does, turning round to check when to sit and when to stand. Not singing, not praying. Just watching and listening. Letting it happen. We're getting towards the end. I've been told what to expect. A curtain will come across. Unseen, the coffin will slide away.

One of the teachers from school walks to the front and starts talking about Rob. School? Are you shitting me? He hated school and school hated him. He was hardly ever there. The teacher's struggling to find something good to say. Words like *lively* and *spirited* spew out of his mouth. Code words. Everybody knows.

There are a few murmurs of agreement as he makes his

way back to his seat. Someone says, 'Well done.'

The vicar thanks him and invites us to pray.

And suddenly I know this isn't right. This service, these people, these words have nothing to do with him.

I find myself walking to the front. I put my hand on the coffin, let it rest there. Then I turn and face the others. Heads that were bowed are looking up now, and the movement ripples down the church. The whole place is quiet. Watching me. Waiting.

'My brother's in here,' I say.

In the front row, Mum's stopped crying. She and Debbie are looking at me open-mouthed. A couple of rows behind I spot Harry, sitting near the teacher from school and a couple of coppers. The rest of the place is packed with kids my age, kids that were never our friends.

I want to tell them everything. The truth. The story of our lives. How it was always me and him, right from the beginning. The beatings we got. The way he looked after me. The adventures we had. The trouble we caused. I want to tell them about Iris and her dog. I want to tell them about Neisha, the girl who changed everything.

I want to tell them about the water, how it took him and how it tried to take me and Neisha. I want to tell them about sounds and smells and sights and pain. I want to tell them about holes in your skull where your eyes should be, marks left by mud that won't wash off. I want to tell them about going mad, so mad you're terrified of a dripping tap. I want to tell them that sometimes the dead don't go quietly. How someone you love can be the person you're most scared of.

I look at their faces. They never really knew Rob. They don't know what happened. Nobody does, except Rob and Neisha and me.

Rob's dead. Neisha's still in hospital.

I could tell them, tell them everything. The truth, the whole truth and nothing but the truth.

Or I could keep my trap shut.

Let it go. Let him go.

'My brother,' I find myself saying, my voice breaking. He tried to kill me, he hated me, but it wasn't always like that. He was the one who wiped my mouth when I was sick. He was the one who slept on the other side of the room, night after night, whose breathing I fell asleep to, whose face I woke up to.

'Goodnight, Rob.'

My words echo in this space and I strain to hear the reply — *Goodnight, Cee.* But it doesn't come. I stand, listening. Lost.

The vicar takes my elbow, shows me back to my seat. He says the last prayer. The organ starts playing and the curtain glides silently around the coffin.

Epilogue

Three months later

The first light sneaks through the gap in the curtains. It couldn't cause me more pain if I was a vampire. It's the start of the day I've been dreading for three months: moving day.

Neisha stirs in her sleep, shifting slightly. Her hand tenses and then relaxes against my chest. I pick it up and bring it to my lips, kissing her fingers one by one.

She opens her eyes and smiles.

'Hello,' she whispers.

'Hello,' I say back.

'What time is it?'

'Just after six.'

She groans.

'You'd better go. Dad'll be up soon.'

'I don't want to.' I hold her tighter.

'I know.' She puts her arms right round me and snuggles in. We lie like that for a minute or so, then she wriggles free and starts to sit up.

'Carl,' she says, 'you've really got to go.'

I don't know how being caught here would make anything worse. She's going, after all, moving a hundred miles away. New job for her dad. New house, new school, new friends, new life.

'Okay, okay,' I say. I slither out of bed and haul my jeans on over my boxers. Neisha stays where she is, drawing the covers up under her chin. I pad over to her window and peep out. It looks like the Arctic outside; it's been cold for more than two weeks and there's been another thick frost. The sky's clear and the sun's about to rise.

'Come with me,' I say.

'Carl,' she says, 'you know I'm going. I *am* going today.'

'I know. Come with me now, just for a walk. It's beautiful out there.'

She looks at me like I've gone mad, then she shrugs off the duvet, and slides her feet out of bed and on to the floor. Her smooth, toffee-coloured legs stretch right up to the hem of her T-shirt. The hint of her soft curves makes me want to fold her up in my arms again, lie down and try to forget the world outside our single-bedded nest.

'Pass me that jumper,' she whispers, breaking into my fantasy. I do what she asks, and while she dresses I put the rest of my clothes on. We creep past her dad's room. The flat is quiet and warm and empty. No clutter. Nothing personal. A temporary place, that's all, a refuge after the flood.

We slip our shoes on and ease the front door open. The cold nearly takes my breath away.

I grab Neisha's hand and we walk to the stairs. Everything is covered in a thick, white layer of frost. It's not ordinary frost. The grass, the trees, and telephone wires are coated in spines of ice, a fringe of needles. It's magical.

'Where are we going?' she asks, her breath ballooning in front of her.

'I dunno. Somewhere with trees, they're amazing like this.'

'The park,' she says.

The grass crunches beneath our feet. We stop to look at a spider's web, its perfect pattern highlighted in ice. More light seeps into the sky, but we can't see the sun yet.

'I'll never forget this,' Neisha says.

'Or me. Don't forget me, will you?' I sound pathetic, needy, but I can't help myself.

'Of course not.'

'Last night …' I start to say. I want to tell her that I didn't sleep a wink, that I spent the whole time watching her, listening to her breathing. That I fell so far in love with her, it was like falling into space. That it was the best night of my life.

'What?' she says.

' … nothing. You were snoring.'

'Shuttup, I wasn't.' She sounds offended, and for a moment I think I've blown it, but she's smiling and she's still holding my hand, and now she starts to lead me down the hill.

'No, I don't think so, Neisha, not there.'

'Someone said it was frozen.'

'I dunno. I—'

'It's all right,' she says.

Perhaps it is. Yesterday, at the inquest, it felt like we were being told it was over. Like that guy, the coroner, was writing 'The End' on the last page for us. It wasn't 'The End', though, was it? It was 'Death by Misadventure'.

An adventure that went wrong.

He said it wasn't my fault. It wasn't anyone's fault. The marks on Rob's ankle showed he'd got caught up in something at the bottom of the lake – wire or reeds or something. That lake wasn't safe for anyone. It could have happened to anybody.

Neisha's still walking a little in front of me, leading me towards the lake. 'It was a sort of ending, yesterday, wasn't it?' she says, as if she's reading my thoughts. 'But now I want to say goodbye. Do it properly.'

The bushes crackle as we push our way through and then we're there, on the edge of the lake. It's perfectly flat today – no waves or ripples, nothing lapping at the bank. We're the only people here, but not the only life. Dotted about, in ones and twos and little groups, there are ducks and gulls standing on the ice, hunched and miserable.

'Come on,' Neisha says.

She inches down on to the ice.

'I don't know,' I say again, but I'm there with her, by her side. There's a surface layer of crystals and then solid ice below. We walk slowly forward. I'm studying the surface, looking for cracks, for I don't know what. The ice isn't all the same: there are darker patches, different shades of grey. I look harder. And in my head, I can see him, Rob, his face pressed up against the underside of the ice, nose and mouth squashed sideways. I see his hands, palms pressing hard, trying to force his way out.

I stop walking.

'I can't, Neisha. I can't go any further.'

A couple of steps ahead of me, she turns round. Her hand has slipped out of mine.

'What's wrong?' she says.

I can't help looking down, thinking of the water

beneath the ice. The currents, the movement, the forces at work. They won't be trapped there for ever. They'll find a way out.

'There are shadows under there … I wanna go back.'

'There's nothing there, Carl. There's nothing there.' She grabs my hand and leads me forward again.

She's wrong, though. The past is down there – memories that will never go away. And somewhere there's a locket. A silver locket that used to belong to a woman called Iris and a chain that once bit into Neisha's neck.

She squeezes my hand. 'Don't look down. Look up. Look all around you. Look up, Carl, and keep walking.'

I make myself lift my head up. The sun's creeping up into the sky now. What was white is now silver, transformed by light. The trees, the bushes, the lake itself.

I slide my feet round so I'm facing Neisha. I kiss her and she kisses me back, then I put my arms round her waist, lift her up and start spinning round. She holds on tight and laughs and I'm laughing too now, the sort of laughter that's next to tears. Don't cry, keep spinning. Keep spinning and spinning and never stop.

Everything starts to blur. The sun's in my eyes and the sky is full of light. The world is full of ice crystals and every one of them is a diamond now, and there are millions and millions of them all around us.

Acknowledgement

John Steinbeck, *Of Mice and Men* (Penguin Classics, 2000), copyright © 1937 by John Steinbeck; copyright renewed John Steinbeck 1965.

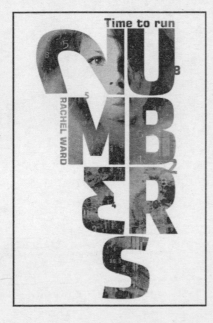